Conyers Street still exists... but you won't find it on any map. It has been consigned to history. But in these pages, you will get to know Conyers Street. And you will get to know the Conyers Street Gang.

You will meet John, Tom, Chrissie and Mary Boden. And you will meet their friends Philly Brown and Gee Gee. Most of all you will get to know about the children who lived through the Second World War through experiences portrayed in these pages.

Welcome to the Conyers Street Gang
Welcome to the Conyers Street Mysteries
Welcome to Conyers Street...

Michael Thame

A Pig Squeal
at Midnight

BOOK BUBBLE PRESS

Published in the United Kingdom by Book Bubble Press

First printed July 2018

Content copyright © Michael Thame 2018

Design copyright © Book Bubble Press 2018

A CIP record of this book is available from the British Library.

ISBN: 978-1-912494-02-6

www.bookbubblepress.com

This book is for my wonderful daughters, Evie and Lily, who provide all the motivation I need to write these stories.

And for my grandfather, Tom Boden, and my grandmother Mary 'GeeGee' Boden (nee Galt), without whom there would not be the inspiration.

Based on real people. Based on real events.

A Pig Squeal at Midnight is the second book of the Conyers Street Mysteries series to be written. However, it is chronologically the first as it is set in the immediate aftermath of Britain's decision to declare war on Germany on the third of September, 1939. In this story, as in real life, our intrepid heroes are evacuated almost immediately. For children from a poor, inner-city area of Liverpool, such as the Conyers Street Gang, being evacuated to a tiny hamlet in rural Shropshire was akin to being sent to a different planet.

The gang suddenly find themselves immersed in a life so different they find it incredibly hard to adjust. But they make friends, they make enemies and they make a nuisance of themselves. Once again, through togetherness and bravery, the Conyers Street Gang shows that the worst of situations can be overcome. They show that children are amazing and that they can achieve anything they want to.

Most of all, they show that together, they are the Conyers Street Gang.

FB @theconyersstreetgang
Insta @theconyersstreetgang

THE
CONVERS STREET
GANG

John

Tom

Philly Brown

Mary

Chrissie

A Journey into the Unknown

"'*This country is at war with Germany.*' That's how he said it, Saranne, just like that." Pop Boden stood in his kitchen, running a hand through his hair. His wife crossed herself.

"Oh, Mary, Mother of God," Saranne Boden whispered, slowly shaking her head.

It was the moment Tom Boden realised something serious had happened. There had been a lot of talk about Hitler and Germany recently, and Tom had always thought it sounded a bit sinister, but things had clearly just changed.

Pop crossed the room and put an arm around his wife. "It means the kids are being evacuated, love."

Tom watched his mother put her hand to her mouth and stifle a sob. She nodded as Pop continued.

"Our John, our Tom, our Chrissie and our Mary. I've been told they'll be kept together."

"When are they going?" Mam Boden asked.

"Tomorrow, love." And Tom saw the tears fall.

*

On Monday 4th September 1939, eleven-year-old John Boden held hands with his two younger sisters; Chrissie aged seven and Mary, who was five. Behind them was nine-year-old Tom, walking beside his mother.

Mam Boden was putting a brave face on things. All the mothers were. Most of the fathers were there, too, as every child made their way to school. That was unusual. Pop almost never took his children to St Alphonsus because he had usually already left to work on the docks by the time the children were ready to leave the house.

But today was very different. Each child carried a pillowcase stuffed with things they would need for the days, weeks, perhaps even months ahead. The Bodens' pillowcases weren't very full. They didn't have much to take with them.

In fact, most of the children on their way to St Alphonsus carried pillowcases with very little in them. Tom carried his brother's and sisters' for them. They weren't heavy.

The Bodens walked to the top of Conyers Street. Tom stopped and looked back at the road he called home. Down at the bottom was a small clearing. It was where he played football with John and his best friend, Philly Brown, who lived on the other side of Conyers Street.

They called it Goodison Stadium because John and Tom were mad Evertonians. Philly Brown supported Liverpool, but they didn't hold that against him. Beyond the clearing was the junction of Great Homer Street where it met with Scotland Road, one of the main roads into Liverpool city centre.

"Come on, our Tom," Pop said softly, but with his jaw set firm. "We need to be on time for your train."

Tom looked down Conyers Street one last time then started along Netherfield Road. On the wall there was a poster; 'Walls have ears!' it said.

Tom didn't know what that meant; in fact, he thought it seemed a bit odd, but he was sure the poster hadn't been there the day before and he was sure Freaky Throupy, on whose house the poster was pasted, would not be very pleased. Freaky Throupy never seemed pleased. It was why the Conyers Street Gang called him 'Freaky'.

The whole of St Alphonsus already seemed to be in the assembly room by the time the Bodens arrived. The headmaster, Mr Smith, was on the stage talking to a couple of serious-looking people whom Tom didn't recognise. Each of the children automatically drifted towards their form teacher; John took his pillowcase from Tom and joined his friends in Mr Gregory's class.

Chrissie and Mary did the same, taking their pillowcases and going to their classes. Tom shuffled slowly towards Miss Marks.

"All right, Tom?" said Philly Brown as Tom approached.

"Yeah. You?" There was none of the normal happy atmosphere that usually came when Tom first met up with his pals in the morning. Gerry Lockhart was there, as was Jimmy Parry, both of them jokers but neither getting up to much. It was noisy in the hall, but it was serious, not fun. No one quite seemed to know what was going on, including the teachers and the parents.

"Ladies and Gentlemen! Can I have your attention, please?" The murmuring stopped as Mr Smith stepped forward on the stage and addressed the room. "As you all know, our children are to be evacuated today given the recent news about Germany."

"As many of you will also know," Mr Smith continued. "Operation Pied Piper has been planned for some time, and the authorities have decided to implement it immediately in Liverpool given the announcement yesterday.

"I have been told that every effort will be made to make sure the school stays together as much as possible, and I have a further assurance that every effort will be made to keep siblings together."

There was a murmur of relief from the parents at this announcement. Tom looked across to his mother and saw her holding a handkerchief to her mouth, her eyes looking red and sore. Pop had his arm around her shoulders, but he, too, looked close to tears, and Pop never cried.

Tom tried not to but felt a tear roll down his cheek. Gerry Lockhart looked at him, opened his mouth but said nothing. Even Gerry knew things were getting very serious.

"The school is to be sorted alphabetically to make it easier for the children to be processed when we get to Lime Street station for the evacuation." Mr Smith moved to his right. "After you say your last goodbyes, can I have all surnames from A through to D lined up here with Mr Farrell, E to I with Miss Marks, J to N with Mr Gregory and O through to Z in a line here with Mr Kynaston. We will be leaving in approximately fifteen minutes. Thank you."

Tom looked at the hall clock. It was nearly nine o'clock. In the sudden noise that followed the announcement, children jostled to return to their parents.

Tom pushed past others and almost launched himself at his mother to give her the biggest cuddle he could. His tears fell freely as someone else, probably John, joined in the cuddle. In seconds Chrissie and Mary were there, too, while Pop told them all that everything would be okay, that the war would be over by Christmas, because that was what everyone was saying. Tom let go of his mother and looked up at her face. She was crying, and so were Chrissie and Mary. John had a very stern look. He was the leader of his little gang, and very soon he would be in charge of keeping them together as they were evacuated to God only knew where.

The call went up from Mr Smith for the children to get into alphabetical order. A few of the mothers tried to stifle sobs, but the children still heard some of their parents' wails of grief, as if they were never to see their children again. Most of the children were calmer; a mixture of ignorance and fear turned them quiet and obedient. As he stood in line next to his brother, sisters and Philly Brown, Tom looked across at the other rows. Gerry Lockhart stood on his own in Mr Gregory's row, looking very nervous. He was an only child and it didn't seem as though there was anyone from his class stood with him. Jimmy Parry was in the farthest row, Mr Kynaston's, standing next to his older sister Alice. He always said he never liked her, but he was very close to her at that moment.

Each of the teachers did a head count. Miss Marks had walked up her row, put a hand on each head, stopped at the end and looked down at a clipboard she held. She then walked back down her row doing the same thing. When she got back to the front, she looked at the clipboard again. Then she looked directly at the Bodens in Mr Farrell's row.

"Philip Heaton!" she said. "Get in this line at once!"

Philly Brown's face fell. He wanted to be with the Bodens, as he was in the Conyers Street Gang and, because everyone called him 'Philly Brown', that was where he stood. But his real name was Heaton. When his mum and dad got married, they moved in with her parents, who were called Brown, and so they were all known as the 'Browns'. By the time they moved into their own house, the name had stuck. Philly hated it when people called him Heaton. He hated it more than ever as he slunk across to Miss Marks' row.

"Before our blessed children go, I think we could all do with a prayer," Mr Smith announced solemnly. The children, in fact everyone in the Catholic school, automatically joined in as the headmaster began with "Our Father who art in Heaven…"

*

It was about two miles to Liverpool's Lime Street station and the children walked in their rows. There wasn't as much chatter as there might normally have been and the children all saw the looks on the faces of grown-ups as they passed them in the street.

Adults stopped and watched as the entire school walked along Scotland Road heading towards the city. To Tom it felt as though there was something in the air that everyone could feel, but no one could see. He didn't like it one bit, and he could see John, Chrissie and Mary didn't either.

Tom was behind them again carrying all their pillowcases as they approached the entrance to Lime Street. There seemed to be children everywhere, even before they got into the station. Policemen were directing the crowds, trying to make sure no children were queueing on the road as the horse carts clacked past and the buses let yet more children off who had come from farther away. The teachers of St Alphonsus did a good job, but then it was a Catholic school, and whenever Tom met children from other schools he always got the sense that Catholic children were better behaved. He soon found out why – normal schools didn't seem to use the cane so much. He was jealous of that.

Once they finally got into the station they were directed to a long row of tables that had been set along the centre of the concourse. The first children in Tom's row shuffled along the tables, holding open their pillowcases. Tom gave John, Chrissie and Mary theirs, then waited in line. When it was Tom's turn, a stressed-looking woman clipped a name tag on him, then a man gave him a large brown case to wear over his shoulder and another man put a brown paper parcel into his pillowcase. Everyone got the same.

"This way, St Alphonsus!" cried Mr Smith above the din as the school snaked its way through the crowds towards one of the platforms where a train stood waiting. Tom had not been on a train very often, but when he saw one he was always amazed by the engines – so huge, shiny and pushing out steam in great noisy whistles and hisses. He didn't have much time to admire it, though, as Mr Farrell started organising his row into the train's compartments. Some of Miss Marks' children came into the same carriage, with some in the carriage behind. Mr Smith stayed on the platform, so it looked as though he wasn't going with them, wherever that might be.

"Philip Heaton!" Miss Marks shouted as Philly Brown scrambled up to the carriage where the Conyers Street Gang sat. He stopped in his tracks and turned slowly. Tom and John looked at each other. They'd rather have Philly with them as well.

"What's this?" said Chrissie as she opened the brown case she had been given.

"It's a gas mask," replied John. "If the Germans decide to bomb us with gas, we need to put that on, so we can breathe properly." Chrissie looked at her older brother. She trusted him. But she didn't like the sound of what she had just heard.

"Our Tom, what are these numbers?" Mary indicated the name tag she had been given. Printed at the top of the tag were the words 'Government Evacuation Scheme: Liverpool' and below that some obvious information: Mary's name, the Bodens' home address, the name of the school. But there were two other things on there as well – 'Code' and 'Party No.' Tom looked at his own name tag; they were the same: the 'Code' was W24/3 and the 'Party No.' was S3.

"No idea." Tom shrugged. "It must be the government or something." John nodded gravely. It usually *was* the government in John's mind. He looked around. The pupils of St Alphonsus were talking a lot more now that they were in their seats on the train.

A number of the boys were laughing at each other because they had put their gas masks on and looked a bit silly. Chrissie didn't like the masks at all, saying they looked scary. In the brown paper parcel they had all been given there was food, more than the Bodens were used to, really. Corned beef, evaporated milk, biscuits, fruit and some chocolate. Mary started to unwrap her chocolate but John stopped her.

"They're emergency rations; you can't just eat them willy-nilly. The government says so." Mary looked hard at her older brother and slowly put the chocolate back, never taking her eyes off him. She was trying to remember when it was that the government told her when she could eat her treats. She didn't think they had told her at all.

With a whistle and a jolt, the train started forward, slowly at first, but gathering pace quickly. Tom marvelled at the patterns on the sandy-coloured rock walls as the train pulled out of Lime Street station and soon after, looked across the rooftops of Liverpool towards the new cathedral.

It wasn't finished yet, and there was still scaffolding all over it, but he could tell it would be enormous, even from this distance.

They had been told not to, but when none of the teachers tried to stop them, many of the children ate the chocolate or the biscuits they had been given. Some even ate the fruit, but no one had a tin opener for the corned beef, not that anyone would eat it.

"Tastes like dog food," John said. Mary continued to stare at him every time she saw someone else eating their chocolate, but Chrissie saw what was happening and whispered in Mary's ear that John knew best. He was leader of the Conyers Street Gang, after all.

Tom was gazing out of the window at the rolling countryside when he felt a sudden tug on his sleeve.

"Made it," Philly Brown said with a big grin. "Miss Marks has been looking at me the whole time, but Davey Pugh has just been sick, so I saw my chance." Tom laughed with his best mate.

They had been friends ever since Philly Brown moved into Conyers Street with his ma and his brother Robbie, who seemed like a Viking to Tom, really tall and really blond with huge muscles he'd got from working in one of the grain stores on Commercial Road.

Robbie had joined the Navy as soon as he was old enough because he didn't like working in a factory. The dust that came off the grain would get in his eyes and they would sometimes puff up to the point where he couldn't see. And some of the stories he told John and Tom sounded horrendous, such as when a cat ran past screaming because it had all these rats hanging off it, biting it. The cat had shot straight out the back of the factory and into the canal to try to get rid of them. Robbie said the cat must have got too close to some rat babies for them to attack it like that. The boys didn't like rats – they were dirty and could be vicious.

"Philip Heaton! Get back here now!" Philly Brown's grin disappeared as he heard the order from Miss Marks once again. Tom gave him a friendly punch as his friend slouched back towards the teacher.

They had been on the steam train for what seemed like ages, passing through stations Tom had never heard of: Nantwich, Audlem, Adderley. It stopped at some but not others when finally Mr Farrell ordered them off the train at somewhere called Market Drayton.

Looking down the platform, Tom could see that Miss Marks' children were also getting off, but Mr Gregory's and Mr Kynaston's did not. They all waved as the train started to pull out of the station once again, taking with it half the children of St Alphonsus.

Once the train had disappeared around a bend, those children remaining on the platform looked at their teachers for news. There was to be another train taking them somewhere different to their classmates who had already left.

"How far are we going, our John?" asked Mary, but her older brother could only shake his head. Further down the platform Tom spotted Philly Brown. He was eating an apple and waved back happily as soon as he noticed Tom looking at him. He liked his food, did Philly. Tom wondered how long his food parcel would last him.

They heard the steam train approaching long before they saw it. Its whistle had sounded a long way off and it was a few minutes before it pulled into the station. It looked just like the first train and they were all ordered on it in much the same way as at Lime Street. Only this time they rode it for just few stops before they all got back off again at a place called Peplow. Again, Mr Farrell and Miss Marks ordered their children into line, and again they watched the train they had been on pull out of the station and disappear around a bend in the track. From where they stood on the exposed railway platform, they could see for miles, and for miles there was nothing to see, other than fields. None of the St Alphonsus children had ever seen so much green.

"My lot this way!" called out Mr Farrell as he led the A to D row out of the tiny station to a waiting bus outside. It said 'High Hatton' on the front and a cheerful looking man sat behind the wheel, smoking a rolled-up cigarette. He beamed at the children as they filed on, and he spoke to one or two, but they just looked blankly at him. They couldn't understand what he was saying.

Miss Marks kept her children on the platform. As the Bodens' bus moved off, Tom caught a glimpse of Philly Brown sadly staring down at them. Tom had been thinking a lot about his mam and pop on the journey, but now he thought about his best friend as well. He didn't think anyone noticed as he wiped a tear away, but John did.

"You're soft, you are," John said, before giving his younger brother a playful tap on the arm. Tom appreciated the gesture, but he was really worried about how long it might be before he saw his family or Philly Brown again. The war was one day old – and he hated it already.

*

"My name is Colonel Gwilt." The man who spoke was a very large man, with a huge moustache that had turned white with age. It turned upwards at the ends, and if it wasn't for the fact that he was in a strange place being looked at by a lot of strange people, John Boden would have laughed.

"I am the headmaster here and it is my job to make you all feel welcome at this very unsettling time." The voice boomed all around the room the Bodens found themselves sitting in. Walls didn't need ears in this case, Tom thought, this man was talking so loudly they could probably hear him in Germany. He wore ridiculous yellow and red checked trousers that were more like shorts, really. In one hand, the colonel held a pipe and in the other, a walking stick. He didn't seem to use either very often. Mr Farrell stood next to him, looking very serious.

"In a moment the good people of this village will come around and talk to you. The idea is that you get to know them and that at the end of the evening you will go with your new family and they will look after you as only a person from Shropshire can. Do I make myself clear?" A few of the adults, most of whom stood near the entrance to the school hall, as if to make a quick getaway, nodded.

"What's Shropshire?" John whispered to Tom.

"Don't know. I thought the village was called High Hatton. It said so on the front of the bus."

"Ladies and Gentlemen, if you would like to talk to these splendid children from Birmingham, Miss Tipton will arrange transfer of papers and you may leave with your new charges."

"We're not from Birmingham."

"What? Who said that? Make yourself known. Now!" Nobody moved. Colonel Gwilt shouted his instruction again, and again nobody moved. The man had gone red in the face and looked absolutely furious. He raised his walking stick and jabbed it in the general direction of the children who sat on the floor. Mr Farrell leaned across to the larger man and whispered something in his ear. The stick came down.

"As I was saying, Ladies and Gentlemen, if you would like to talk to these fine children from Liverpool…" Gwilt stood where he was, observing everybody in front of him. His trousers seemed to move on their own, even though there was no wind in the room. The children of St Alphonsus were sitting in small groups or by themselves. If there were siblings, they sat together. If a child was on his or her own, they sat on their own. The Bodens, all four of them, were the largest group.

Slowly, one or two of the adults who had been by the entrance door walked amongst the children, looking down at them. Tom watched as a white-haired woman walked straight towards one of the girls sitting alone.

"I'll have that one," she said, loudly, pointing a bony finger at Kitty Connor. "Well, girl, come along. What's the matter with you?" Kitty looked absolutely petrified. She often played with Chrissie and Mary at school, which was unusual because she was in Chrissie's class and not many people played with children in other years. All the other children watched on, frightened at what might happen next.

"It's all right, Kitty, you will be absolutely fine with this lady." Mr Farrell crossed the room and held out his hand to the young girl on the floor. Slowly, she took his hand and got to her feet, her eyes flitting from her teacher to this new, scary woman she had never met before.

"I am Miss Hoof," the old woman said, saying 'Miss' in that way that some old women seemed to do.

"My name is Kitty Connor," the girl replied.

"Come along, then," the old woman said. "I've baked you a cake, and I don't want it to burn." Kitty smiled, not because of the cake, which she was sure would be lovely, but because Miss Hoof suddenly didn't seem nearly as scary as she had just a few moments ago. She picked up her things and went with her new guardian to fill out Miss Tipton's forms.

With Miss Hoof having gone first, the other adults seemed to become a bit more confident and they all started to walk around the seated children. Tom didn't like it one bit, and he could tell John didn't either. Every time someone approached the Boden children, they would look at the group and walk away again.

"It's like being a slave, waiting to be picked," Tom whispered to John, who nodded his agreement.

"I hope we get someone good," John replied, saying what Tom, Chrissie and Mary were all thinking.

The whole process seemed to last forever, and the number of available children grew fewer and fewer until there were just the Bodens left. Mr Farrell came over.

"I'm sorry, John. It looks like no one has got the room to take all four of you at once. Colonel Gwilt thinks you will have to be split up."

"No!" John leaped to his feet. "Mr Smith promised our mam and pop that all the families would be kept together. You can't lie to them like that." Tom jumped up as well; then Chrissie and Mary did the same. Mr Farrell was shaking his head.

"I'm really sorry, but Colonel Gwilt and Miss Tipton tell me there are only two other families who are still meant to come. One says they can take two and the other says three. I'm told they live quite close together, so when they come, it will be easy for you to stay with Tom and for Chrissie and Mary to stay with the other family." John shook his head. Tom could see he had clenched his fists. Surely John wasn't about to hit his own teacher? There'd be Hell to pay.

"Our John, if what Mr Farrell says is true, then we'll have to do that," Tom said.

"The only other option, I believe, is that you would all fit in Colonel Gwilt's house." Each Boden child felt the air flow out of them. They looked across at the huge man with the enormous moustache, daft trousers, the pipe and the walking stick that looked like a weapon in his hand. The thought of living with the headmaster filled them with terror.

"Okay, we'll agree to be split up," John said, "as long as we're always allowed to play with each other whenever we like. I've got to look after my gang – I mean, my sisters."

Mr Farrell smiled. "Well done, John Boden. That's the spirit."

Just then the door to the school hall burst open and a tall young man crashed in with a dog at his heels, followed by a small woman whose hair was tied in tight buns covering her ears as if they were permanently cold. Everyone in the room looked in the direction of the commotion.

"Sorry we're late," the man said, raising a hand. "Bloody sheep made a run for it, din' it?"

John and Tom both smiled. They liked the man instantly. His face was red and when he looked more closely, Tom could see he was filthy. The woman following him was spotless, but it was clear she was nervous. Tom wondered whether it was because she was scared of being told off by Colonel Gwilt or because she was suddenly going to have at least two new children in her house.

"Don't worry about a thing, Fred," the colonel said. "Just four of them to go, and then we can all go home."

"But we can only take three," the little woman said. "Tell him, Fred, we can only take three. There's no way we can take four."

"And don't you fret, Mrs Bytheway, we've got it all sorted," the colonel said a little more softly. John and Tom giggled at the name, then stopped when they saw Fred Bytheway staring at them.

"The Bettons can take two, so you'll only be needing to take two yourself." Colonel Gwilt pointed his pipe at the Boden family. "What'll you be having? Boys or girls?"

The hall doorway opened again, and another flustered-looking couple burst in, trailing a young red-headed girl with a face full of freckles.

"Sorry, Colonel," the man said. "Our Meg decided to go hiding in the woods again." The red-headed girl looked more angry than embarrassed.

"It's okay, Alf, with you here now, and Fred and Molly here as well, you two can decide which of this lot you want." Colonel Gwilt was much less scary when talking to the adults, Tom noticed. He didn't seem to bark his words quite as much as he had when he had instructed the children.

"Two brothers and two sisters; all the same family, and promised they wouldn't be split up, but there isn't anywhere else for them to go, so you and Fred have got the choice."

The two men shook hands and said their helloes. The women smiled at each other, then all four walked towards the Boden children. The Boden children stared back, as if ready to defend themselves at a moment's notice.

"What with you having your Meg, Alf, maybe it makes sense for you and Lily to have the two girls?" Fred Bytheway suggested. Alf and Lily Betton nodded, as did Molly Bytheway, but Meg Betton rolled her eyes. All the children saw it; Chrissie and Mary decided they didn't like her at all and suddenly wanted to stay with the Bytheways.

"Makes sense to me, that, Fred," Alf Betton replied. "What do you reckon, Lily, love?" Lily Betton nodded her agreement and both Bettons turned to look at their daughter, who stood with arms folded, deliberately staring at the floor.

"Meg?" Alf Betton said, but the red-headed girl didn't answer. "Right," said her father, "we'll take the two girls. Good luck with the boys, Fred. Now, where do I sign?"

As Alf Betton went over to Miss Tipton's desk, Lily Betton introduced herself to Chrissie and Mary. The Boden sisters were polite as ever, but neither took their eyes off Meg Betton. She looked a bit older than Chrissie, maybe as old as Tom, and they could see she was trouble. John and Tom also studied the girl. So far as they were concerned, she had been rude to their sisters, and they weren't having that.

"Fred Bytheway." John and Tom's new guardian had his huge hand outstretched for the boys to shake, a beaming smile on his face. "And this is my wife, Molly."

John took responsibility, as leader of the gang. "My name's John Boden," he said. "And I've been told we are allowed to play with our sisters whenever we like."

"Is that right?" said Fred, shaking John's hand. He looked across at Tom. "And this is?"

"Oh, that's our Tom, by the way."

Fred laughed. "Don't be silly, he can keep his own name."

John looked at Fred for a minute, then noticed Tom giggling beside him as he shook Fred's hand.

"I think we'll get on fine, don't you, Molly?" Fred said, and the small woman next to him beamed. Tom liked their new guardians already. John was still wondering why Fred and Tom were giggling.

18

"What's your dog called?" asked John, trying to sound important.

"She's called Ella," Fred Bytheway replied.

"That's a strange name for a dog," John said.

"Named 'er after my mother. Just to annoy 'er, like," Fred Bytheway winked and smiled. Tom giggled some more.

*

The Bytheways and the Bettons and the Bodens left the school in High Hatton together. Meg Betton walked slowly behind the group. The adults kept excitedly saying things to the Bodens, asking them about Liverpool, what it was like where they lived and what was different from where they were. Fred Bytheway, a farmer, told the boys about the things he did most days. John and Tom couldn't believe they were going to live on a farm. And Tom couldn't stop stroking Ella. She was a beautiful chocolate brown colour and had a brilliant white chest. He thought she must be a collie. Lily Betton kept telling Meg to catch up with her new friends, but the red-headed girl kept her distance. Chrissie and Mary gave knowing glances to each other. They could tell they were going to have to sort this new girl out. Or John and Tom would, seeing as she was older.

The group travelled along a country lane with hedgerows so high no one could see over them. After five minutes they came to a fork in the road where the group split. The Bodens said their goodbyes, giving each other hugs and promising to see each other every chance they got. The Bytheways and John and Tom took the left fork. Chrissie and Mary went with the Bettons and took the right fork.

None of them knew that someone was watching.

The Colonel's Violin

Meg Betton woke early. It was light outside and already quite warm as she lay in her bed looking up at the ceiling. She was furious. Her mum and dad never listened to her. First of all, she didn't want anyone sharing her bedroom, and when it became obvious that it would have to happen, they ignored her and picked the girls instead of the boys. She didn't like girls. They wanted to play with dolls or hopscotch or any other number of silly little girly things that bored her. She wanted to climb trees and to run about. She was even good at football and was always the only girl playing. She liked that.

But as she lay in her bed trying to listen to the birdsong outside her window, all she could hear were the little sighs and snores coming from the other side of her bedroom where two complete strangers were fast asleep. The whole thing was unfair and annoying. Her dad had tried to explain why other children had to stay in her house, but she still didn't see why she should have to give up her nice, big bed or that she should have to sleep in the tiny camp bed he had put in her room.

"There'll be two of them, Meg," he had said after he had unfolded the rickety metal-framed bed with its thin and knobbly mattress.

"They should sleep in it!" she shouted back. Her bed was *her* bed and no one else's. Why should anyone else get to sleep in it? And why should she have to sleep in such a rubbish replacement?

She also didn't think it fair that her mum had made her take clothes out of her wardrobe and stash them under her bed, just so that those other girls could put their clothes in there. She had a mind to put her own clothes back seeing as the two new girls only seemed to have brought a single change of clothing each. They didn't need all that room. One of the new girls coughed, annoying Meg even more. She huffed and turned onto her side, punching her pillow before closing her eyes to try to get to sleep in the lumpy bed.

*

Tom Boden knelt on his new bed with his elbows resting on the windowsill. He couldn't quite believe what he was seeing: ducks and geese. Or at least he *thought* they were ducks and geese. Then there were chickens, loads of them, walking and pecking around a dusty yard. A wooden barn filled with hay formed the right-hand side of the yard, while to the left there was a long, low brick building with a flat roof. He wondered if it might be a stables, but he couldn't see any horses. At the far side of the yard a red tractor was parked by a wooden gate that led out into a huge field where sheep were eating grass. Tom couldn't see where the field ended as it fell away, but he wondered if there was a river down there.

A dark wood bordered the field to the side and back, with steep wooded hills beyond. If he craned his neck to the left and looked over the roof of the stables, he could see a mansion on a hillside in the near distance. It was a curious building, square, but three storeys high, and with a roof that sloped into the middle from all four of the sides, ending in a tall central chimney stack. It almost looked as though it wasn't quite finished, but it was still big enough to house the whole of St Alphonsus School.

John moved somewhere behind him. There were two beds in the room and, because he was older and also because he was leader of the Conyers Street Gang, John decided he should have the double bed. Tom didn't mind at all. At home the two of them shared a single bed and Tom increasingly noticed how his older brother was getting bigger and taking up more room. It never crossed his mind that he was getting bigger as well. He was nine and a half now and had just spent his first ever night outside of Liverpool. It felt strange.

The night before, Aunt Molly, as she insisted on being called, had made a lovely stew with loads of meat in it. It was better than his mam's Scouse, but then most things were; Tom was the only one in his family who wouldn't eat that stew, even when it had lamb in it. After they had their tea, and were feeling really full, John and Tom talked to their new family about life in Liverpool. Uncle Fred in particular seemed to hang on every word. He said he liked where he lived but sometimes it was a bit quiet and boring. It had only just gone dark outside when the boys started yawning. It had been a long day. Uncle Fred showed them up to their new bedroom and said goodnight. As he gazed out over the beautiful scene before him, Tom couldn't remember a night he'd slept so well. Not for the first time that morning, he wondered how his sisters were getting on.

*

"What would you normally eat for breakfast in Liverpool?" Lily Betton asked as Chrissie and Mary tucked into eggs and toast. They each had a glass of milk and had barely come up for air since the plates of food were placed in front of them. Chrissie swallowed.

"Bread and dripping most days, Mrs Betton."

"Really? You don't have eggs, or milk, or bacon?" Chrissie shook her head as she chewed on another piece of lovely thick toast. "Goodness. And please, call me Aunty Lily. Mrs Betton sounds so formal!"

Meg scowled at the two girls opposite. She didn't like the fact that they had slept so long and that once they finally decided to wake up, they had talked quietly to each other without saying anything to her. Then, when they had all gone downstairs for their breakfast, her mum embarrassed her by sending her out to get eggs from the small brood of chickens they kept in their back garden. She had lost her bed, most of her bedroom and now she was out getting their breakfast. As soon as she could she was going into the woods, *her woods,* to get away from them.

"Meg, love, once the girls have finished breakfast, can you take them to the Bytheways' house where their brothers are, so they can all go to school together?"

"Mum! They can find their own way! They just need to walk back the way they came last night. Even those two couldn't get lost!"

"They are guests in our house, Megan, and you will take them to the Bytheways." Chrissie and Mary looked at Meg. Her mother kept her back to them as she fussed about in the sink. Meg stuck her tongue out and Chrissie and Mary did the same. Meg might be older, but there were two of them and they were used to fighting.

As it happened, the boys turned up at the Bettons' house just as the three girls were about to leave. Molly Bytheway was with them, but she stayed to talk to Lily Betton as Meg sulked and dawdled in taking the four Boden children to the school.

She could have just stomped off, though, as children were appearing from almost every house in the tiny village, all walking in the same direction. The Bodens could easily find the school. Instead, she stayed just close enough, so they could see how little she liked them.

"She's really nasty, our John," Chrissie said quietly. "She's complained about everything we do, like where we are sleeping or what we are having for breakfast or showing us where the toilet is."

"I can't stand her," Mary added. "She sticks her tongue out all the time. If she keeps doing it, we're going to have a fight."

"If there's going to be a fight," John warned, "make sure me and our Tom are there. She's bigger than both of you."

"I'll have her," Mary snarled through gritted teeth. John smiled at his younger sister. She might be little, he thought, but she definitely had the Boden spirit.

Tom had been listening carefully. He thought it a real shame his sisters hadn't had the same kind of experience he had had in High Hatton. After being the last to be picked in the school and the scary thought of living with people he had never met before, the Bytheways really were very nice people. Uncle Fred and Aunt Molly seemed to have gone to lots of trouble for them, sitting and talking to them in the living room with the fire on, even though it was quite warm, and giving them lots of hot milk to drink. And then there was Ella. She was never allowed in the house, but Tom had never had a dog before and he adored her. The Bytheways had made Tom feel really at home. He missed his mam and pop and his other brothers and sisters terribly, even though it was just one day since he had last seen them all, but the Bytheways made him feel so much better.

He didn't think John thought like that, although he knew he was also missing the rest of the family in Liverpool.

Tom just thought it was a shame that Chrissie and Mary had been put with a girl who sounded really awful. He didn't like girls fighting. It didn't seem right, somehow.

The four of them filed into the same room they had been sat in the evening before, to find it packed with children. Tom wondered where they had all come from as the village seemed so tiny. Surely they couldn't all be living there? Colonel Gwilt was on the stage again, and looking stern again, with Miss Tipton standing just behind him. Another woman closed the main door and the chatter from the children stopped the moment the colonel spoke.

"Damn bad business, war. It has no place in a civilised society, but Hitler is no civilised man." Colonel Gwilt paced from side to side across the stage, the children's heads moving in unison. Miss Tipton was doing the same.

"I fought the Germans," he continued, with many of the boys suddenly interested, "and I have fought the Boers and I have fought the Dervishes of Sudan. What I have seen I wish none of you will ever see. War is a terrible thing. I can only say that I am delighted that our great nation and government has decided to protect our future generations by sending you to places like this, to High Hatton, where you might be spared the horrors of war should Hitler decide to bomb England."

Mary looked around. She was getting bored. War might be terrible, but war seemed very far away at the moment and that meant it wasn't interesting to her.

The Bodens were in the front row, so Mary had to crane her neck to look up at the colonel as he paced across the stage. She turned to look at the children behind her instead and tried to see where Meg was. Only she couldn't, because Meg was nowhere to be seen. But she had walked in front of them to the school and then she had gone straight in, hadn't she? Mary looked again, more carefully. She definitely wasn't there, and her deep red hair would really stand out, wouldn't it? She turned to Chrissie.

"Meg's not here," she whispered.

"Silence!" The word came like a roar. Colonel Gwilt had been at the far side of the stage when he had shouted, but now he was rushing across to the source of the noise. He banged his walking stick down and pointed his pipe at John, Tom, Chrissie and Mary. "I will not have children speaking when I am speaking! Which one of you was it? Raise your hand! Now!"

His face became redder as his voice rose with each word he uttered until he almost seemed to scream out, "Now!" Tears immediately welled in Mary's eyes. The colonel was terrifying. John wanted to put himself in front of his little sister, but he was so shocked by the shouting he dared not move. Every other child in the room was stunned and really glad it wasn't them the colonel was shouting at.

"Come on! Who was it?" He banged his stick down again, the pipe in his other hand quivering. Slowly Mary raised a hand. She was openly crying, but she was also brave, and she did not want anyone else in her family getting into trouble. Colonel Gwilt took a deep breath. The colour faded from his cheeks and he lowered the hand that was holding the pipe. He pointed to a door on the far side of the stage.

"Go to my room and wait for me there." His voice had become much softer and quieter as he quickly calmed back down. He had gone from normal to hysterical and back again in seconds. It was quite a performance. No one in the room made a sound as Mary got up and hurried across the front of the stage to the closed door Colonel Gwilt pointed at. Standing there, she saw every face in the room staring back at her as tears rolled down her cheeks.

The colonel resumed his speech and the children observed him pace from side to side as if they were watching a game of really slow tennis. None of them dared look away in case the headmaster turned on them.

But Mary had been right; Meg was not there.

*

Colonel Gwilt had walked off the stage and taken Mary into his office. The door slammed shut behind them. John, Tom and Chrissie were really worried for their sister. The colonel was a terrifying man, and Tom in particular wondered if he wasn't a bit mad. The three of them kept looking at the closed headmaster's office door as Miss Tipton and the other lady, who had been introduced to them as Mrs Doody, began separating the children into two groups. The older children were to be taught by Miss Tipton, whereas the younger ones were to be taught by Mrs Doody, who wasn't a teacher but had offered to help with all the new arrivals. It meant that, once again, John and Tom were separated from Chrissie and Mary.

There was an ear-piercingly loud screeching sound coming from the headmaster's office. Everybody suddenly stopped talking.

Some of the children on Miss Tipton's side of the room nearest the headmaster's office put their hands over their ears. Some others, who Tom thought might be local children, were smiling and laughing. Apart from them, almost everyone else, including Mrs Doody, was totally confused by what was happening. Then, as suddenly as it had started, the screeching stopped, and the door slowly opened. Mary walked out and quietly shut the door behind her. She stared back as everyone looked at her.

"You will be with me, child," Mrs Doody said, breaking the strange silence, and Mary went over. Chrissie stepped out and put her arm around her little sister, John and Tom looking on anxiously. But Mary seemed okay. In fact, she was smiling, and then some of the children in her group started to laugh as well. John and Tom were relieved, but they desperately wanted to know what had just happened in the headmaster's office.

*

As it happened, they didn't have all that long to wait. Miss Tipton told them that they were only there to get sorted into their new classes and that school would begin properly tomorrow. It wasn't quite break time when they were all let out.

"He played the violin."

"He did what?" John asked, as Mary explained what the piercing sound coming from the colonel's office had been.

"He played the violin," Mary stated again. "Only before he started, he told me why I was in so much trouble and then he told me how he was so bad at playing the violin that he used it as a punishment. So that's what he did. It hurt my ears."

"I thought you were going to get the cane," Chrissie said.

"So did I," Mary said, "but he told me he thought hitting children was wrong."

John whistled.

"I wish they thought like that at our school," Tom said, the others agreeing with him. St Alphonsus was a great school and the teachers were mostly very good, but you got told off for almost anything and the teachers were always ready to get the cane out if they felt like it. John was forever getting caned and Tom had had his fair share of putting his hand out ready for the stinging pain. The palms of his hands always felt like they were on fire for ages afterwards.

"Anyway, our John," Mary continued, "I'm going back to our house to see where Meg has got to. She's so nasty. I'm going to tell her mother that she's skipped school."

"No one likes a snitch, our Mary," Tom said. "What's she going to be like if you start telling on her?"

"I don't care," Mary argued. "She's horrible. Anyway, I want the chocolate that our John wouldn't let me eat yesterday."

"But they're emergency rations. You should only eat them when there's an emergency." John's protests fell on deaf ears. Mary had had a strange morning and she didn't care what her older brother thought. They had had a really good breakfast, so as far as she was concerned, there wasn't going to be an emergency.

The Bodens parted at the fork in the road, promising to meet back at the Bettons' house in an hour. On the short walk to their new house, Chrissie tried to change Mary's mind about telling on Meg. She agreed with Tom that it might not be a good idea, but Mary seemed determined.

By the time they had got to the house and gone to their bedroom, Mary herself started to have doubts and decided she would ask Meg where she was, then threaten to tell Aunty Lily unless Meg started being more nice.

"Hey!" said Chrissie. "What have you done with my pillowcase, our Mary?"

"I haven't done anything with it. What do you mean?"

"It's not where I left it in the wardrobe." Chrissie showed Mary the space in the bottom of the wardrobe where she had put her pillowcase. Immediately, Mary rushed to the bed and looked under her pillow. Her pillowcase was where she had left it, but when she looked inside, all her food had been taken.

"She's pinched it!" Mary exclaimed.

"Who? Meg?"

"Yes, Meg! She's gone and done it now. I'm telling Aunty Lily right now."

Mary stormed out of the room and down the stairs, with Chrissie hurrying after her younger sister.

"Aunty Lily?" Mary shouted. "Are you there? Aunty Lily?"

"Out here!" came the reply. Mary ran through the house and out the back door. Aunty Lily was hanging washing on the line. By the time she got there, Mary was a little out of breath.

"Meg's taken our food. She didn't go to school and now she's pinched all our chocolate and biscuits and things."

"Slow down, dear. What do you mean she didn't go to school?" Mary could have kicked herself. She had decided she was going to keep that secret so she could threaten Meg with it, but she'd forgotten and said it anyway.

"I mean," Mary looked at Chrissie, who shrugged. "I mean that she took us to the school, but then she disappeared and she wasn't in the classroom when Colonel Gwilt was talking to us."

Aunty Lily frowned. It wasn't like Meg to play truant. "And what's this about food?"

"We came back to eat our pillowcases," Chrissie said, "but when I went to get mine from the wardrobe, it wasn't there. And when Mary found hers, the pillowcase was there, but all the food had gone."

"It's Meg – she's pinched it all," Mary blurted out.

"I doubt that, Mary," Aunty Lily said. "She's many things is my Meg, but she is no thief."

"But she is!" insisted Mary. Aunty Lily's voice grew firm, and the girls recognised it.

"My daughter is no thief. She has been brought up properly. I will ask her if she knows anything when she gets back, but until then I don't want either of you saying that again, even to your brothers."

"But—"

"No buts, Mary. She may be strong-willed, but you will not call her a thief."

"Who's a thief?" Chrissie and Mary spun around to see Meg in the doorway to the house.

"Meg, dear, do you remember the pillowcases Chrissie and Mary arrived with yesterday?" Meg nodded. "Do you know where they are now?"

"They put them in my wardrobe, I think. Why?"

"They aren't there now. The girls are just wondering whether you had moved them." Meg looked at Chrissie and Mary, then back up at her mother. She suddenly realised what was happening.

"You think I took them?"

"I'm not saying that, love, I am just asking if you know anything about them."

"You think I am a thief? How could you, Mum?" Meg looked really hurt and Chrissie felt sorry for her.

"Then where is our food?" Mary shouted. Meg looked again at her mother, started to shake her head, then ran back into the house. Aunty Lily shouted after her daughter, but she was out the front of the house and off down the street in a flash.

"Told you it was her!" Mary said almost triumphantly. Aunty Lily turned on her.

"Don't be such a silly girl! Meg is not a liar and she is not a thief. You saw how upset she was. I'm telling you now, do not say another word to anyone about this until you see Meg and apologise."

Mary thought about arguing, but she saw Chrissie shake her head and thought better of it. She sighed.

"Aunty Lily, someone has taken our food, and Meg has been really horrible to us and she didn't stay in the school and, and…" Mary looked at the ground. "I'm sorry if I've upset her, I just really wanted to eat my chocolate."

Aunty Lily smiled and patted Mary's shoulder. "I understand, love. Meg will be back, and we can all say sorry to her then. I know you don't think so just yet, but she is a good girl. She's just been a bit confused by this evacuation lark. It doesn't just affect you and your family; it affects all of us here as well. That will be why she didn't go to school. I'll have words with her about that, but in the meantime, I've got some cake in the larder, if you want some?" Chrissie and Mary did not need asking twice.

*

John and Tom were walking back to the farmhouse when they heard the unmistakable sound of football. They headed through a gate into a field neighbouring the Bytheways' farm and saw a game in full flow. Tom counted; it looked like it was five against four.

"Do you think we could join in, our John?"

"Course. Why not?" John said. "Got room for two more?" he shouted as one of the goalies went to fetch the ball. Everyone else stopped and looked at them.

"Are you any good?" one of the boys shouted back.

"I am," John replied. Then he looked down at Tom. "And he's all right, I suppose." Tom gave his brother a hurt look and punched him on the arm.

"In that case, you play on my team because we're losing. He can go on the other side." The boy came towards John and Tom and shook hands with them. He had a big mop of blond hair.

"Ted Edwards," he said. "From Birmingham. We all are." John and Tom introduced themselves, Tom suddenly realising why Colonel Gwilt thought they too were from Birmingham, before Mr Farrell had corrected him.

The other players had come over and names were exchanged. The goalie who had fetched the ball kicked it high in the air to restart the game and Tom suddenly found himself marking his older brother. John always played up front and reckoned he was the next Tommy Lawton, Everton's great centre forward who had scored all the goals last season. Everton were champions, and John and Tom had managed to sneak into Goodison Park for most of the home games. Philly Brown sometimes came too. When Liverpool were playing at home, Tom used to go with him to Anfield, but John refused. He hated Liverpool.

34

Ted Edwards launched the ball towards John, with Tom sticking close behind him doing his best impression of Billy Cook, Everton's defender – and Tom's idol.

John spun around and knocked his younger brother flying as he controlled the ball and hit an unstoppable shot inside the far post, which was really a small tree. The ball went miles, and the goalkeeper gave John an unimpressed look as he ran after it.

"You pushed me," Tom moaned as he picked himself up off the ground.

"Don't be daft, our Tom," John said. "You got on the wrong side."

"Great goal!" Ted Edwards came running up to John and patted him on the back. "You really are pretty good! You can tell who the player is in your family." John laughed, but Tom was really unhappy.

"Edward Edwards, is it?" Tom asked. "Your mum and dad only know one name?" Ted Edwards stopped laughing. He was older than Tom, probably the same age as John, and about as big as well.

"The first son is always called Edward in my family," he said, quietly, staring hard at Tom.

"Leave it out, our Tom. Ted's done nothing to you."

Having fetched the ball, the goalkeeper hoofed it downfield and all arguments were off as the game got underway again. It was a fairly even contest between the teams and there were some good players on both sides. As he always did, Tom tried his hardest, but he never got the better of his older brother, who started smashing the goals in from everywhere.

The boys left the match when they saw Chrissie and Mary waiting by the gate for them. The girls had gone to the Bytheways' farm where they found Aunt Molly in the kitchen making sandwiches.

She had asked them to go and find their brothers and bring them back for their lunch. John and Tom promised Ted they would return as soon as they could and left the Birmingham boys playing in the field.

Despite her promises, Mary couldn't wait to tell John and Tom what had happened about their pillowcases of food and Meg storming off as she did. Chrissie had to remind her that, because Meg had reacted in the way she had and rushed off, she thought Aunty Lily was probably right. It sounded fair enough to Tom, but John was less certain.

"If we find her, she's for it," he said.

They didn't have to wait long. The four of them ate their lunch in the Bytheways' kitchen, all washed down with milk, and then rushed back out again. Aunt Molly's cries of "digest your dinner!" went ignored.

Tom had to rush back to the privy when he suddenly got stomach pains. He always did when he ran straight after eating. But he loved football so much, he just couldn't stop himself. When he went back to the match the second time, he got a shock. There was another player on the pitch; it was Meg. And she was brilliant.

John had joined in with the game, but Chrissie and Mary, as per usual, were not interested. However, what was unusual was that they actually watched the match, and that was because Meg Betton was playing. She had joined the side Tom had been on, and, so far as Tom could tell, she looked like the best player on the park. She was super fast and had incredible close control.

Tom kept watching; she even had the beating of John, who was just too big to keep up with all of Meg's agile little movements.

Tom had never seen anything like it, and, as she bore down on goal, leaving three of her opponents on their backsides, it seemed as if they had never seen anything like it either. She sent the goalie the wrong way. The only player still standing on the other team was Ted Edwards, and he had his hands on his hips staring in wonder at the girl with the long red hair who had just scored such an incredible goal.

"How did you learn to play like that?" John said, looking bemused.

"There's not much else to do round here," Meg gasped. "So I've spent hours practising against walls. It's the one good thing about you lot being here; it means I can have a game."

"And you really didn't take our food?" By now Tom, Chrissie and Mary had joined John and Meg. Chrissie had asked the question.

"No I didn't," Meg said curtly.

"Then why have you been so nasty to us?" Mary cried. "We haven't done anything nasty to you." Meg looked at the floor and thought about the last twenty-four hours. How her mum and dad insisted they had to take people in because the government said so. She did like boys more than girls, but was it fair she took it out on Chrissie and Mary? And if their food had gone missing from what was her bedroom, of course she'd be the most likely to take it. Chrissie and Mary weren't to know how honest she was.

"I didn't mean to be, not really," Meg said. "I'm used to being on my own, and when I was told other children were coming to stay, I didn't really like it. It's my house and my mum and dad. I don't want to share it or them. I'm sorry. I promise to be nice from now on. I would like my bed back, though."

Chrissie and Mary looked at each other and smiled. "I'm sure we can sort something out."

"Good!" It was Ted Edwards who had spoken. "About time we got this game back on the go, don't you think? Tom, you come on our side, I think we're gonner need you now that Meg turns out to be the new Alex Massie."

Meg smiled and Tom thought Ted's comment was spot on – he remembered watching Alex Massie when Aston Villa had come to Goodison Park for the last home game of the season. Everton had won 3-0 and his all-time hero, Billy Cook, had actually scored. It had been a great match. But Alex Massie had been brilliant day, even though he was on the losing team.

Tom went into defence, as usual, and spent a great deal of the afternoon failing to keep up with John. He got really annoyed after a while and tried to foul him, but John just laughed as he got out the way of his wild lunge. "You need to be quicker than that!" John shouted as he scampered away and scored again. It was now turning into a bad day. Tom didn't like losing. Meg had arrived too late to change the course of the match.

Chrissie and Mary were asked if they wanted to join in, but neither of them liked football at all. Instead, they sat on the grass by the side of the pitch and made daisy chains. They didn't often get the chance to in Liverpool, as there wasn't much grass around and the stadium at the bottom of Conyers Street never grew that many flowers. Each of the girls wore daisy crown and had another chain easily as long as John by the time Molly Bytheway shouted that tea was ready. She stood by the gate and called for all of the Boden children.

"You too, Meg Betton. I've agreed it with your ma."

John and Tom groaned, but the Birmingham lot agreed to call it a day with a rematch planned for the same place tomorrow. Meg was full of high spirits as she skipped across the grass towards the gate. Chrissie and Mary were trying carefully to pick up the daisy chains they had made. Molly Bytheway had already headed back to her house to serve up dinner – another delicious stew full of lovely, meaty goodness. She decided the city children looked unhealthy compared with Meg and the other local children. Maybe they didn't get enough fresh air, she thought, or enough good, healthy food? While they were there, she had decided, they were going to get as much countryside goodness as she could provide.

John and Tom waited by the gate for their sisters. Meg joined them and tried not to sneer as Chrissie and Mary walked through with their daisy chains. They were just too girly for her. She closed the gate behind them and looked out across the field that had just been their football pitch. The far end was bordered by trees and, as she looked, she saw some movement.

"Did you see that?"

"See what?" John and Tom said together.

"There's someone in the woods down there." Both boys stared in the direction Meg was looking but could only see trees. "I saw them there earlier," Meg added quietly to herself. The boys shrugged again and started towards the Bytheways' farm. Meg followed, but she was right. Someone had been watching them.

And he was still watching them.

MEG'S DEN

The Stranger in the Woods

Tom opened his eyes and blinked. The sun streamed through a gap in the curtains and shone right on his face. He turned away. In the other corner of the room was John, his chest slowly rising and falling as he slept contentedly in the massive bed.

He didn't have a watch, but Tom knew it was early. He lay there thinking about Mam and Pop, and about his brothers and sisters he had left behind when the four of them had been evacuated. He thought about Liverpool and how he missed his life there. He thought about a lot of things that upset him while he lay there quietly, and when he moved he realised his pillow was damp.

He hadn't noticed, but he had been crying. He wiped his nose on the sleeve of his pyjamas and sat up. John always said big boys didn't cry. But then he had seen John cry on occasion, so maybe neither of them was big enough just yet.

Tom shrugged. It didn't matter. It was okay in his opinion to cry about your family if you missed them as much as he did. He didn't care what John said. What he *did* care about was his tummy. He was starving, which he immediately thought odd because they had had such a big tea the night before. People in the countryside definitely had more to eat than people in the cities, and he wondered if that was fair.

"Biscuits," Tom said quietly to himself, before walking across to the chest where he'd put his pillowcase. He hadn't eaten any of his rations, because John had told him not to, but with the amount of food Aunt Molly was giving them, he didn't see any likely emergency. He lifted the lid; the pillowcase wasn't there. He had put it right on top of a load of old and yellowing newspapers, but it had gone. Tom looked across at his brother. John wouldn't nick his rations, would he? He had only made a small attempt at hiding his things, putting the pillowcase in the chest when John wasn't looking, but he trusted his brother not to take anything even if he did find his things by accident.

"Our John."

"Hmm?"

"Our John! Wake up!"

John stirred. "What is it?"

"My rations have gone. Have you had them?"

John opened his eyes and looked at Tom, standing with the chest lid open.

"No, I haven't. I didn't know where you'd put them."

"So who's had them, then?"

John rolled over to go back to sleep. "Dunno."

"Where are yours?"

The older boy stretched out his arm and patted the other pillow in the double bed. "Here," he said, then sat bolt upright, lifting the other pillow in one swift movement. "Hang on! Mine's gone too!"

The brothers looked at each other, trying to understand what had happened. Who would walk into their room and search long enough to steal their rations? Neither had been hidden very well, but whoever it was must have been looking for the pillowcases.

"Meg was here last night. She even had tea with us. You don't think she would have had the time to come in and pinch them, do you, our Tom?"

The younger boy shrugged, thinking. It made sense in that she'd been in the house and Chrissie and Mary thought she'd taken their rations.

"Would be a bit obvious, don't you think?" Tom said. "She's already been accused once. Maybe she thought she'd got away with it and decided she could do it again?"

"It must be her, then," John stated. "I'm going to have her."

"Hang on. Remember how hurt she was when Chrissie and Mary accused her? I don't think that was put on. She seemed properly upset."

"Who else could it be? It can only be Uncle Fred or Aunt Molly and I can't think they would need to do that. They've got loads of food."

*

The boys mentioned the missing pillowcases at breakfast. Aunt Molly insisted the boys were not to accuse Meg, saying there was no way such an honest girl would sneak into their room and steal anything. John tried to protest but Aunt Molly was having none of it. She said she'd speak to Uncle Fred when he came in for his lunch to see if he knew anything. The boys were disappointed. That meant waiting a few hours before they might know anything. They walked to school grumbling and met the girls at the fork in the road.

"Have you pinched our rations?" John said, marching straight up to Meg.

43

"Our John!" Tom gasped. "You heard what Aunt Molly said." Chrissie and Mary looked at Meg, who looked back at the four Bodens. She sighed.

"No, I didn't," Meg said.

John looked at the ground. "Sorry. I didn't mean to say it, it just came out."

"So your chocolate's been taken too?" Chrissie asked, and the boys nodded. "That's a bit of an incidence."

"Coincidence," Tom corrected.

"Shut up, clever clogs!" Chrissie shouted back. Tom ignored her.

"Aunt Molly's going to ask Uncle Fred when he gets in later," he said.

"You don't think it's him, do you?" Meg asked.

"Of course not," Tom said. "It's just that he may have moved them or something and put them somewhere we don't know."

"But why would he do that?"

"I don't know, Meg. But if it wasn't him, and it wasn't you, and we would hardly steal our own things – who could it be? And why would they only be pinching our rations in a house where there's loads of food in the larder? It doesn't make sense."

The four of them agreed with Tom. It didn't make sense. But even in Liverpool, in the middle of a big city like that, people didn't lock their doors. They certainly wouldn't lock them in a tiny hamlet like High Hatton. Anyone could just walk in.

*

School was much the same as the previous day. The children separated into two classes; the older ones with Miss Tipton and the younger ones with Mrs Doody.

44

One of the boys from Birmingham got sent to the headmaster's office and the screeching, ear-piercing sounds started soon after the boy had closed the door. Definitely better than being caned, Tom thought, but it did have the disadvantage of making everyone's ears hurt. With caning it was just you who felt the pain.

John and Ted smiled at one another. They were immediately best pals and were a lot like each other. Tom didn't like it. He was used to having John to himself. At home, John didn't really have any friends outside his gang, because he took looking after it so seriously. The screeching stopped, and the boy came back out of Colonel Gwilt's office rubbing his ears. The whole school giggled.

"Silence!" the headmaster screamed from behind his closed door.

School finished at lunch and the children left for home. John had told Ted about their missing pillowcases, and Ted said he would ask around his Birmingham lot to see if anyone knew anything. As they parted at the fork in the road, they agreed to meet back up for football as soon as they had eaten, which would take up about five minutes because they wolfed their food down so quickly.

They were back in the field in no time, although Tom had to suddenly rush back. He wished he had listened to Aunt Molly as she shouted at them to digest their food before running off. He never learned. By the time he returned, the teams had been picked, and the game had started.

John and Ted were team captains; Tom slotted into defence on John's team and immediately watched Meg fly past him in a blur of long red hair as she scored the first goal. John looked at his brother in disgust.

He had obviously forgotten how good she was the day before. There was no stopping her, and the only way to win was to simply score more goals than she did. Tom would boot the ball up to his brother in attack and, more often than not, he would score. But every time Meg got hold of the ball, she did score. She was winning the game on her own. The goalie on Tom's team hoofed the ball up field after another Meg solo effort, only he sliced it wide.

"Wass goin' on 'ere, then, eh? Beaten by a girl?" Tom turned to see a boy of about fifteen standing a few feet away, holding their ball. He had a leery grin across his spotty face and seemed bald, although looking more closely, Tom saw the boy's blond hair was just cut really short. There were two other boys with him and they too were leering. They also had really short hair. Tom hadn't noticed them arrive, but suddenly the atmosphere seemed a whole lot worse. These boys looked like trouble.

"Shut up, Colin Rickers!" Meg shouted. "I'd beat you an' all, so don't go mouthing off." The leer disappeared.

"What did you say?" Rickers took a step forward.

"You heard her," John said, also taking a step forward. Ted did the same. Rickers laughed.

"Like that, is it? Sticking up for your girlfriend?" John and Ted looked at each other. Rickers laughed again. "You are! Brilliant!"

"Just give us the ball back." Ted stepped forward again, this time with his hand out. Rickers seemed to think about it.

"Erm, no," he started. "Me and the lads fancy a kickabout, so I think we'll just take it if that's all right, eh fellas?" Rickers' mates smiled. Ted took a further step forward, and John did the same.

"Give us the ball back," Ted said again, more firmly. "Or I'll—"

"You'll what? Want another kinda beatin', do ya?"

Ted launched himself at Rickers, hoping for the element of surprise. Rickers *was* surprised, but not so much that he didn't have just enough time to drop the ball and swing his arm at the smaller boy. John rushed in as well, and Rickers was struggling, but when his two mates joined in they turned the tide back in his favour. Rickers, Ted and John were a flailing mass of arms and legs rolling on the ground. Rickers' mates were at his side, aiming punches at Ted and John. Quickly, Tom and the rest of the boys saw that they needed help and every last one of them leapt in.

From behind them a police whistle sounded. It stopped everyone immediately. Tom was amazed how quickly he had got there – surely no one could have called him in that time?

"What's going on here, then?" They all stood up. Ted had ripped his shirt and John had a fat lip, but Rickers had a swollen eye. It looked sore. Someone had caught him with a good one.

"He stole our ball," Ted said, panting.

"Yeah," John added, "and then he started fighting Ted."

The policeman raised his hand. "A Brummie and a Scouser? In High Hatton? If there's any thieving going on it won't be by a local." Ted and John looked aghast at each other.

"But—"

"Shut up!" The policeman stopped Ted. "Give me the ball, Colin." Rickers did as he was told; picked up the ball and handed it to the policeman. "I'm taking this," the policeman said.

"But PC Purslow, Ted is telling the truth. He did steal our ball."

47

"Meg Betton, I suggest you stop hanging round with this lot," PC Purslow sneered. "You'll probably catch something. Now I am taking the ball, so you lot clear off!" The policeman turned and started back towards the gate. Rickers and his mates followed a short distance behind. Ted, John, Meg and Tom all watched in horror as the policeman threw the ball to Rickers, before getting on his police bicycle and riding away. Rickers looked back and waved the ball in the air.

"That's not right, that," someone said.

*

With no ball to play with, Ted and the rest of the Birmingham boys wandered off. Someone suggested they tell Colonel Gwilt what had happened, but Meg said he wouldn't do anything. Instead, they agreed to see if they could find another ball from somewhere.

"Do you reckon those boys are the ones who stole our rations?" Mary asked. She and Chrissie had joined the boys and Meg after PC Purslow and Rickers had gone. They had seen what had happened from a distance and dared not move until everything was over.

"I don't know, Mary," Meg said. "Rickers has always been a bully, but I doubt he'd risk getting found in my house or in Fred and Molly's. He's a coward."

"Can we all play something together, then?" Chrissie asked. She and Mary never liked football and always went off on their own when a match started. They were used to it in Conyers Street, but they were in the countryside now and everything was a bit unfamiliar. They wanted to be close to their brothers.

"We can play hide and seek," Meg said. John and Tom groaned. "We can play in my woods," she continued, pointing to the trees at the bottom of the field.

"Okay," John said, suddenly interested. "But we'll play war instead of hide and seek. Me and Meg versus Tom, Chrissie and Mary."

"Why am I on the girls' team?" Tom asked.

"Before we play war, we will play hide and seek," Meg insisted. "My den's in there and I don't reckon you'll be able to find me."

"You've got a den?" John asked, and Meg smiled.

"Yes, and it's a good one."

They were all interested in that. A den sounded really exciting. Chrissie wondered if it had furniture ("It's even got a bed," Meg replied.) and Mary wanted to know if there were any small spaces she could climb through. Meg wasn't so sure, but she did point to all the trees they could climb up.

Mary was happy with that. When they got to the edge of the woods, Meg stopped and told the Bodens to count to a hundred.

"I will be on this side of the stream," Meg said happily. "I promise you I am in there, but I bet you can't find me!" With that she shot off through the undergrowth and vanished amongst the trees in seconds. John was suddenly bored; he didn't like waiting and the sound of Mary counting was getting annoying, even though she had only reached twenty.

He stepped forward to the edge of the undergrowth and peered in. He couldn't see Meg anywhere.

"She's disappeared already," he said. "We'll go on fifty." But Mary didn't even get that far. On forty-one they all heard a girl's scream.

"That's Meg," said Tom, bursting past his brother and into the woods. John was straight in after him, then the girls. They all sprinted towards the sound of screaming, John overtaking Tom as they got nearer and nearer. Suddenly Meg shot out from behind a bush, and she was being chased by a boy. John gained on him easily and within a few strides grabbed the back of the boy's shirt. He swung out with his other arm, hitting the boy on the head. Tom arrived and rushed to Meg, who was crying. He looked back. The boy was crouched down, holding his hands protectively above his head as John continued to hit him. There was something familiar about him.

"Stop it, our John," Tom said, letting go of Meg and rushing back to where his brother was. He grabbed John's arm and pulled him away. "Stop!" John did as Tom asked and stepped away. The boy slowly lowered his hands and stood up. He had a big grin on his face.

"Philly Brown!"

"You hit like a girl, John!"

"*I'll* hit you like a girl in a minute," Meg said angrily, the lines of tears visible on her face. She turned to John and Tom. "You know this idiot?"

"We do," Tom nodded. "He's my best mate in Liverpool."

"Then what's he doing in my den?" John, Tom, Chrissie and Mary all looked around. They couldn't see a den.

"I can explain," Philly said, the grin disappearing as he saw how much he must have frightened the red-headed girl. "I'm sorry I scared you, but I really can explain."

"You'd better." Meg wiped her face on her sleeve and pushed past Philly Brown, who was suddenly feeling wretched. It wasn't good to upset a girl. The Bodens followed Meg. They all wanted to know where the den was, and they wanted to know why Philly Brown had been in it. Meg walked straight up to a huge bush between two large trees and pulled some of the foliage to one side.

"In here," she said, then disappeared. As he got closer, John could see a slight gap in the leaves. Pulling the foliage aside, as Meg had, revealed a shed. There was a path to the right-hand side which he followed. The shed had a little veranda and stood right beside the stream. It was why Meg had said not to cross the stream; she'd be easy to spot from that side, but from this side, her den was invisible.

The inside of the shed was like a bedroom. There was a small bed along one side, a couple of chairs and a table. There were even some books on a little bookshelf that immediately caught Tom's eye.

"This is brilliant," Chrissie said.

"Start talking," Meg said, looking furious. Philly Brown stood in the doorway and felt awkward. Mary had sat down on the bed, as had Chrissie. Tom and John were still standing.

"This is my pillowcase!" Chrissie squealed, holding up the empty sheet of pale blue fabric.

"And this is mine," Tom said, holding up a white one. "I recognise where the stitching has come undone."

Once again, all eyes were on Philly Brown. He was nervous. He thought he might get thrown out of the Conyers Street Gang, and he'd gone through a caning to be a member.

"Right," he started. "I followed you here when we all got off that train."

"But that was two days ago," Tom said. "You can't have been out here all that time. What did you eat?" Philly looked at the pillowcase in Chrissie's hand. Everyone realised what he meant.

"Oh," said Mary.

"When you got on that bus," Philly continued, "I saw that it was going to some place called High Hilton."

"Hatton," Tom said.

"Whatever, I saw the name on the bus then watched it drive off. I noticed a road sign, and it said High Hatton was one and a half miles away. So I thought, *I could run that*, so when Miss Marks wasn't looking, I sneaked off. I sprinted all the way here and saw your bus parked outside the school, so I waited.

"You came out and I followed you until you all split up. I didn't know who to follow until I saw the girls turn into their house, so I decided to go there.

"There's a shed in the back garden, with the chickens," Philly Brown said. Meg nodded, still angry, but less so now she was hearing this new boy's story.

"So I ate my rations and kipped down in there. I got the shock of my life next morning when you came out to get those eggs from the chickens. I was sure you would see me."

"You weren't sleeping with the chickens?" Meg scowled. Mary giggled.

"I was."

Meg shook her head.

"When you had gone, I sneaked out the shed and hid in the woods at the bottom of your garden.

"I didn't know what I was going to do, but I was hungry, so when I saw you all go off to school, and then I saw your mum come out of the house, I thought I'd sneak in to see if I could find Chrissie's or Mary's rations. I didn't want to steal from your family, Meg, because I thought that would be really bad, but I thought my friends would understand when I told them."

Philly Brown stopped and looked at the faces in front of him. He was desperate for one of them to forgive him.

"But I like chocolate," Mary said quietly. "I don't have it very often."

"I'm sorry, Mary. You know I only did it because it was an emergency."

Mary nodded.

Philly Brown gave a sigh of relief. "Anyway," he continued, "so I found your rations and went back to the woods. I was eating an apple when I next saw you, Meg, so I decided to follow you. I only found where you had gone when you came back out of the bush hiding this den. When I saw there was a bed, I decided to stay here that night.

"A bit later on I heard loads of voices and knew it was a football match," Philly Brown looked at John and Tom. "I thought you two would be playing. You weren't to start with, but then I saw you arrive. I watched you when that woman called you in for your dinner and saw where you were staying. Are those ducks or geese in the farmyard, Tom?"

"I think there might be both," said Tom. "I don't really know."

Philly Brown nodded. "I saw you both rush back to the match and then watched you rush back to the privy like you always do, Tom." John and the girls laughed at this. Even Meg smiled.

"So you were both playing footie and that woman came out soon after you and went off towards the village, so I saw my chance to get hold of your rations, too, John and Tom. I'm sorry I took them, but I was really hungry again.

"I came back down to these woods and watched Meg beat all of you at football. You're really good, by the way." Meg blushed. "And then it was night time. Not that you would know it round here, the amount of noise going on over at that other farm last night."

"What sort of noise?" John asked.

"Oh, a van turned up and then there were some squealing pigs, I think. Surprised you didn't hear it."

Tom shrugged. "Maybe we were asleep."

"Well, the van drove off the other way out of the village, and I came back here. It took me ages to find this den in the dark." Meg smiled at this. She was very proud of the hideaway she had built with her dad the summer before. She even spent whole nights out there sometimes.

"And that's it, really. The next thing, you find me in here, scream the place down and I get jumped by John. I wasn't really expecting that."

Philly Brown thought he had won over his audience. He had told John, Tom, Chrissie and Mary that he had stolen from them and that he had been stalking them all around the village for the last two days. He had also told Meg how he had sneaked into her house and slept in her shed and den without asking.

He had done a lot of naughty things, when he thought about it, but all because he wanted to be with his friends and back in his gang.

"What happens now?" he said, looking at Tom, as was everyone else.

Tom didn't like being put on the spot like that. They all thought he was dead clever, and he knew he was a little bit, but he had no idea how you went about telling grown-ups that Philly Brown had run away from Miss Marks' class and been hiding in the woods ever since.

"We'll have to tell someone," he said, eventually.

"Colonel Gwilt," said Meg.

"No!" said Chrissie quickly. "He'll eat him alive!"

"Why don't we take him to Aunt Molly?" John said. "I reckon she'd know what to do."

Tom agreed, as did the girls. Philly was suddenly very nervous again. What if he got sent back to Miss Marks? She'd kill him, for one thing, but all this effort to stay with his pals would be for nothing and being taken from them would be the worst punishment of all.

*

The six children went out of the woods and across the field where the football match had taken place. Philly Brown had been telling everybody what it was like sleeping out in the open, and all the strange noises he heard in the countryside at night. The Bodens hung on his every word when he talked about hearing what he thought were owls hooting. Meg nodded, but it was nothing new to her. She had lived all her life in High Hatton and had heard all the noises Philly Brown was describing many, many times.

"It was a fox," she said when Philly mentioned a terrible high-pitched cry – like a baby screaming in agony – he had heard. Mary thought this sounded horrible.

Everyone was laughing as they turned into the yard of the Bytheways' farm. Philly Brown had just described the number of times he had to wee during the night because the sound of the running stream just by the den made him need to go. But the laughter was suddenly cut short.

"Hello children!" Molly Bytheway was carrying a milk urn across the yard towards the farmhouse when she saw the Conyers Street Gang and Meg. "I've not seen you before," she said, eyeing up Philly Brown. "Is this a new friend or one of the ones from Liverpool?"

"Liverpool," Tom said quickly, then went silent. None of the children said anything else, which made Molly Bytheway suspicious.

"Right," she said. "And what's your name?"

"Philly Brown," Philly Brown replied. Again, everyone was quiet.

"Is there something wrong, Philly Brown?" the woman asked. The children looked at each other then all ended up looking at Tom. He was the best at talking to grown-ups, even though John was the Conyers Street Gang's leader.

"The thing is, Aunt Molly, Philly isn't supposed to be here."

"Oh?" she said. Tom kicked at the ground.

"He's our best friend and, and, well... he was meant to be staying somewhere else."

"What do you mean?"

Philly Brown took over. It was his mess, so it was up to him to explain. "I was meant to go with Miss Marks to somewhere else, but I didn't want to be away from my friends, so I sneaked off when she wasn't looking."

Molly Bytheway looked at the children before her. They all looked back, a mixture of curiosity and concern etched on their faces.

"So you shouldn't be in High Hatton at all?" she asked, and Philly Brown shook his head. "I can't believe they haven't missed you," she muttered, almost to herself. "And you've been where for the last two nights?"

"I slept in Meg's shed and then in her den," Philly Brown said.

"And what did you have to eat?"

"Rations." Philly Brown looked at his friends. "I had lots of rations." Molly Bytheway thought for a moment.

"So it was you who took John's and Tom's rations?" Philly looked at the ground. Even though his friends had forgiven him, it didn't sound any better when he heard the words again.

"Oh, dear me! You must be half starved. Come in, Philly Brown, I'll sort you some food." With that, Molly Bytheway turned on her heel and went towards the kitchen door. The children didn't quite know what to do and stood still for a moment until Meg grabbed Philly by the arm and marched him towards the farmhouse. "Come on!"

"I can do you a quick bacon sandwich, but then I'm going to have to go to Colonel Gwilt and explain what's happened. Do the rest of you want bacon sandwiches?" All the children nodded. The food in High Hatton was the best the Conyers Street Gang had ever had, and in seconds they all sat around the kitchen table as Aunt Molly fried the meat. The smell was heavenly, and Philly Brown in particular felt his mouth watering at the thought of eating hot food.

"Hello!" Fred Bytheway entered with a cheery grin. He closed the door on Ella, leaving the dog outside. He had been out in the back field feeding his sheep and his shirt was soaked through with sweat. He looked very dirty. "You're a new one," he said, noting Philly Brown. Molly Bytheway explained the situation to her husband, whose smile faded the more she spoke. "All a bit serious, that," he said. "You all right, lad?" Philly Brown nodded. "So we're gonna tell old Gwilt, are we? Probably best. Can't have a missing child wandering the countryside, 'specially not a city lad like yourself." Uncle Fred ruffled Philly Brown's hair.

"You heard what's happened up at the Hoggins' farm?" Fred Bytheway said to his wife as the children started tucking into their bacon sandwiches. "'E had a pig rustled last night, 'e reckons."

"I know, Fred. I had PC Purslow up here this morning wanting to talk to you about it."

"Why's he wanna talk to me about it?"

"He's just fishing," Molly Bytheway said. "I fobbed him off, told him you was off out getting some feed for the geese." Listening to the Bytheways, Tom realised a couple of things that suddenly fell into place; firstly, that it wasn't just the children who disliked PC Purslow; the Bytheways did as well. He wondered what history there must be for his adopted family to speak about the policeman as they were. The second thing he realised was the missing pig.

"Aunt Molly and Uncle Fred," he said, "I think Philly might have heard them taking that pig last night." Fred Bytheway stared at the small boy.

"Out with it, then," he said.

"Well," Philly Brown began, "I needed a wee last night because it's murder trying to sleep next to a running stream." Mary and Chrissie giggled again. "And so when I went out of the den, I heard all these squealing noises, so I went to have a look. I thought it was coming from here to start with, then I realised it was the next farm."

"The Hoggins'," Fred Bytheway said knowingly.

"So I went to take a closer look. I walked past here, and I saw this van and a few blokes and heard squealing. Then the squealing stopped, and the van drove back down towards the road, so I dived into a hedge, but I needn't have as it went the other way. I didn't think much of it."

The Bytheways exchanged glances. "How many blokes?"

Philly Brown shook his head. "I don't know really. It was hard to make them out in the dark, but it was more than one."

"And what about the van? Did you see what sort it was?" Philly Brown shook his head. Horse and carts were more common in Liverpool, although there were more cars and buses these days. Even though Philly was interested in motor vehicles, it had been too dark to see much at all.

"And no markings or names on the side?" Fred Bytheway asked. Again, Philly Brown shook his head. He had only seen the outline. He had no idea what colour it even was. Fred Bytheway looked again at his wife.

"Reckon we tell Purslow this?"

"Just tell Gwilt, I reckon," Molly Bytheway said. "He can decide what to do. I'm taking Philly up there in a bit to see what the colonel thinks we should do with him."

Philly's face fell, and Mary gasped. Put like that, they all realised Philly Brown was probably going to be sent back to Miss Marks. The bacon didn't taste quite so nice after that.

*

Philly Brown went with Fred and Molly Bytheway up to Colonel Gwilt's house, which turned out to be the big mansion Tom had seen from his new bedroom window. Meg and the rest of the Conyers Street Gang stayed at the farm. Chrissie and Mary were amazed when Meg showed them how to carve soap into really clever shapes. She was very good at it and created a beautiful swan out of one bar of soap. She told the Bodens she'd learned how to do it at Girl Guides, something Chrissie and Mary could never go to. There wasn't a Guides troop near Conyers Street, and Mam and Pop would not be able to afford the uniforms even if there was one.

"I didn't think you liked girly things like that," John said.

"It's not girly," Meg replied. "It's not easy, you know. I bet you couldn't do it. And anyway, Girl Guides isn't just about being a girl and just doing baking and things like that. We go on camps and things, make rafts in case you get shipwrecked at sea. I wouldn't do it if it was just doing 'girly' things."

John thought better than to argue. He gave Tom a nudge and left the girls to their soap. The boys went outside into the yard. They'd not really had a proper look yet. There were the ducks, or geese, roaming around freely, and the chickens were constantly pecking at things on the ground. They went to the back field and looked at the sheep. There weren't many, maybe twenty.

"Blimey!" John said. "How ugly are they?" The sheep seemed big to the boys. They had seen pictures before, but they seemed much larger in real life. "Looks like they're wearing a judge's wig," John persisted, laughing.

"I wonder if they are all the same breed," Tom said. They *did* all look the same, he thought, with thick, short, creamy-coloured coats but black faces and legs where the wool didn't grow. And it was true it looked like they had judges' wigs on, but Tom thought they looked impressive. The only thing he didn't like was the matted tails they had, which looked really dirty. He wondered if they had lots of diseases because their bottoms must never be clean.

John and Tom soon got bored and were poking around in the barn when they heard voices coming from down the road. Colonel Gwilt's deep growl was loudest, and that must mean Philly Brown was with him. The boys ran out to see Gwilt, Philly Brown and the Bytheways heading towards the farm. Philly looked pleased and broke into a run when he saw his two friends. Ella the dog ran alongside him, barking excitedly.

"I can stay!" he shouted, jumping up and down. The Boden brothers were ecstatic. Meg, Chrissie and Mary came running out of the house as they had heard Philly's shout; they didn't want to miss anything.

Gwilt stopped when he reached the smiling children.

"Now look here, Brown," he began, his voice getting higher with every word. "What you have done is very, very serious." Philly Brown's smile vanished. He was looking alarmingly at the pipe the colonel brandished. It seemed to be getting closer and closer to his face so that he wasn't sure he wouldn't be stabbed by it.

Fred and Molly Bytheway looked on. They had experienced Colonel Gwilt's telling-offs when they had been pupils at the school. Fred smiled to himself as he realised Philly Brown probably didn't know about the violin torture yet. He thought it a fair bet that Gwilt would call Philly in first thing next morning to give him a screech.

Colonel Gwilt finished by saying something about getting the official paperwork from someone. Philly looked blankly at him but nodded as if to show the headmaster he was listening and that he understood. The colonel barked a final "Right!" then turned and marched towards the school.

"What did they say, Philly?" Chrissie asked.

"He just made a couple of phone calls and said it was okay for me to stay if somewhere could be found for me. Luckily, Mr and Mrs Bytheway said they had room for one more, so I'm staying here." John and Tom cheered. "Thank you," Philly Brown said to the Bytheways.

"You're welcome," said Molly Bytheway. "And don't call us Mr and Mrs again. It's Uncle Fred and Aunt Molly. John, Tom, you'll have to share that double bed now that Philly's having the smaller one. Is that all right?"

John and Tom were more than all right. Back in Liverpool they slept in a single bed. Even with the two of them in the double bed John had been sleeping in on his own, there would probably be room for three or even four more children.

Just then a roar went up and the boys and Meg realised a new football match was starting in the field. They looked at Molly Bytheway, who smiled.

"Off you go," she said. "And straight back when I call you for your tea!"

The foursome ran off down the lane. Fred Bytheway called Ella back when she started to run with Meg and the boys. The dog looked disappointed, which is how Chrissie and Mary felt. They looked at each other and sighed. It was boring watching the boys and Meg play football.

"How about we go to Meg's den?" Chrissie suggested. Mary readily agreed, and the two of them started on their way to the woods by the football field.

Fred Bytheway put his arm around his wife's shoulders as they watched the two little girls wander up the lane and go through the gate.

"Reckon Gwilt will do 'owt about Philly seeing the pig theft?" he said.

"Dunno," Molly Bytheway replied. "Ain't nothing to do with us, now, is it?"

"No, s'pose not," Fred Bytheway agreed. He kissed his wife on the top of her head and told her he'd be back in time for his tea.

THE BYTHEWAYS' FARM

Life on the Farm

At school the next day, Philly Brown got a shock. Firstly, he had to stand in the headmaster's office while Colonel Gwilt gave him an extra-long session of screeching violin. He was shocked because he had no idea what was coming, but John and Tom grinned as he went back to class rubbing his ears. Philly got another shock when, just before school was to end at lunchtime, Miss Marks appeared, looking very angry. Philly Brown's smile vanished. Suddenly he was back in the headmaster's office with his teacher from Liverpool, who was obviously not happy that he had run away.

Lunch came, and John and Tom waited for Philly Brown outside. Normally they would be straight off to the football field for another game with Ted Edwards and his Birmingham boys. More often than not, Meg would play as well, which meant whichever side she was on usually won.

Philly Brown came out of school with his teacher and he looked nervous. Miss Marks stared at John and Tom then stormed past them. The woman looked furious. She got on a bicycle and rode away.

"What happened?" Tom asked.

"She told me that when I get back to Liverpool I'm going to be caned every day for a month."

John and Tom whistled. That was really harsh.

"She wanted to cane me today, but Colonel Gwilt wouldn't let her. She was amazed when he said he didn't own a cane, and she hadn't brought one. He told her that he had already disciplined me, but I didn't know what he meant."

"It's the violin," John said. "That's how he punishes people." Philly Brown nodded, as if he understood, but really he was thinking about a month of caning. It would hurt.

"Anyway," Tom chimed in, "we're going to be here for ages yet. I bet she'll have forgotten by then."

"How long do you reckon the war's going to last, John?" Philly asked the eldest boy.

"Dunno. I've heard Uncle Fred say it will be over by Christmas."

Tom nodded. He had heard much the same as well.

"Do you think that's long enough for Miss Marks to forget?" Philly Brown asked, nervous.

John and Tom shrugged.

"Still," Tom said, "that's a long time for us not to see Mam and Pop, our John, and a long time before we see Vera and Brian and Tony. In fact, it's a long time before any of us see Conyers Street again."

The three boys were quiet as they passed along the lane towards the football field. It was September. And Christmas sounded an awful long way away.

*

As it was, the time passed quite quickly. They had endless games of football and loads of fights with Rickers and his gang. The same happened each time; they were playing football and Rickers tried to steal the ball. Then there would be a big fight between Rickers' lot and all of the boys playing football before an adult would see what was happening and put a stop to it all. It was usually Uncle Fred or Aunt Molly because their farmhouse bordered the football field.

Sometimes PC Purslow was around and he never changed. He always took Rickers' side and the footballers had to go and find another ball.

Meg always spoke up for the evacuees as the one local child who usually played, but whatever she said always fell on deaf ears. As soon as they heard the police whistle, everyone knew they were about to lose the ball. PC Purslow obviously loved winding up the visitors. He was absolutely horrible.

He even refused to do anything about Rickers when he tried to steel some of Tom's sweets. Once a month a man with a van drove into High Hatton and he would sell sweets. All the children loved sweets, and the Bodens and Philly Brown always made sure they had plenty of pennies left for the sweet van man.

If anything, the van had more sweets in it than Mrs Hann's sweet shop back in Liverpool. But the difference was the children liked Mr Teece, who brought the van round. They never liked Mrs Hann, who would always try to short-change them when they bought their sweets from her.

It was after one visit by Mr Teece that Tom got jumped on by Rickers and his gang. Because he liked sweets more than anyone else, Tom had decided to queue up and wait for the van to stop one Friday afternoon while the rest of the children were out playing.

He needn't have bothered as no one else showed up early and he was the only one there when Mr Teece arrived. Acid drops and troach drops were his favourite, and he made sure he had plenty of each, but he also decided to have a bit of liquorice for a change. He loved the sherbet dip that came with it.

Tom went back towards the fork in the road, passing the Bettons' house, although Meg, Chrissie and Mary were nowhere to be seen.

He thought they must be in the woods, probably in Meg's den, and wondered if they'd remember the sweet van came that day. He turned right at the fork, heading towards the Bytheways' farm when someone grabbed him roughly from behind and spun him around.

It was one of Rickers' cronies, the one called Yapp, leering and baring a toothy grin. Tom tried to run from the much bigger boy but found his path blocked by the other crony, Yale, who stopped him in his tracks. Then Rickers stepped out from behind a tree and Tom was really worried. He was probably a bit far from anyone to shout for help, not if he didn't want to get bashed first, and there was no way he could outrun any of them, even Yapp, the really fat one.

"You're one of them Scousers, aren't you?" Rickers said, sneering. Tom didn't answer. He'd been in scrapes like this before, surrounded by boys who wanted a fight.

But in Liverpool, they were usually his own age and he always gave as good as he got. This was different. They were all much bigger than he was.

"Give us yer sweets, and we won't bash you," Rickers said. Tom didn't have many options as the three boys had him trapped in the middle of the road. The only thing he could think of was the tree Rickers had stepped out from behind.

If he pretended to make a run for it but instead climbed up the tree, he might have a chance of getting away. It worked.

Tom looked one way, shouted, "Wha's tha'?" and, as Rickers and the other two looked around, he was off and straight up the tree. Tom didn't stop climbing until he heard Aunt Molly shouting. When he looked down, he saw Rickers, Yapp and Yale walking slowly in the direction of the village. He'd managed to escape.

But then he had to get down and that wasn't so easy. As he reached with his foot for a lower branch, his hand slipped, and he fell right onto a goat that had been grazing in the field under the tree. The goat let out a panicked scream and ran off.

Tom lay there, holding his leg, which he had managed to scrape as he fell. It was bleeding freely. Aunt Molly took him home to clean him up. When she then took him to see PC Purslow, the policeman said there was nothing he could do, as Rickers and his gang had not actually stolen anything. Aunt Molly was livid.

Fortunately, Purslow did not appear too often as High Hatton was so tiny that he was only ever there when something had happened, and that was usually a pig being stolen; it happened three times at the Hoggins' farm.

They had been really unlucky, Uncle Fred said, adding that it was the black market and people would pay lots more for meat now that rationing had started. That did not make sense.

The Bodens and Philly Brown had never seen so much food. There never seemed to be any shortage in High Hatton. Tom wondered how Mam and Pop were coping back home in Liverpool.

He found out three weeks after they had been evacuated, when Pop suddenly turned up at the Bytheways' farm one Saturday evening.

The boys were out playing football and, for a change, Meg was playing with the girls. John and Tom couldn't run fast enough when they saw their dad standing at the gate at the top of the field with Uncle Fred and Aunt Molly. Philly Brown ran the other way to get Chrissie and Mary. When they arrived, they were very emotional; they had so many questions for Pop.

Tom felt tearful as they had not seen any of their family for what seemed like ages. Somehow the letters Mam and Pop kept writing always left them feeling worse rather than better.

Uncle Fred couldn't believe it when Pop said he cycled all the way from Liverpool after working on the docks until lunchtime. The farmer got a map out and Pop tried to work out how far he had ridden that day. He thought it was about sixty miles, maybe more.

"That's miles," John whistled, then got offended as everyone laughed at him.

"And when are you heading back?" Uncle Fred asked. He nearly fell off his chair when Pop told him he would be heading back the next day. "That's some effort," he said, his admiration for Pop clear to all the children present.

So, Pop stayed the night at the Bytheways' farm. He slept in the single bed in the boys' room, Philly Brown joining John and Tom in the big double bed.

Aunt Molly had made another big dinner for everyone, with Pop telling her how happy and pleased he was that his boys seemed to have been put with such a nice family.

Tom thought about being away from his parents often and he realised how awful it must be for them as well. He understood that John, Chrissie, Mary and himself were all much safer in the countryside, but how awful must it be to miss half your family like that and still have to worry about the Germans bombing you?

Of an evening, when they sat in the Bytheways' living room, they would sometimes hear the unmistakable low hum of aircraft engines. Tom was adamant every time that they were German bombers and they were going straight for Liverpool. They were the times he was at his lowest.

John seemed to be able to blot out any of the really nasty thoughts, but Tom could never get away from the image of their house in Conyers Street getting bombed.

He usually cried himself to sleep when they heard bombers overhead at night. He was as quiet as he could be, because he didn't want John to know, but his older brother could hear the little sobs and, on occasion, cried a little too.

It was a horrible time.

*

Just like he said he would, Pop went back to Liverpool late the next day. Double summer time meant he could leave after tea and arrive in Conyers Street just as it got dark. But the light was worse the next time Pop visited a couple of weeks later, and he had to leave earlier.

Soon, Tom realised, he would have to leave quite early on the Sunday if he was to be able to see where he was going.

The one time he didn't ride his bike to High Hatton, Pop got the train because he brought Mam, Vera, Tony and Brian with him.

The Boden children were beside themselves with excitement. Tom watched closely as his mother walked slowly around the Bytheways' house, running a finger along surfaces to check Aunt Molly's dusting was up to scratch. Mam took a lot longer to say she was satisfied with the farmhouse her boys were staying in, or that they were being well enough fed and looked after by the Bytheways. It was a bit harsh, especially on Aunt Molly, Tom thought, but he understood why his mother behaved as she did.

They had been apart as a family for almost two months now, and she wanted to make sure all was well for all of her children. No doubt she had been the same at the Bettons' house where Chrissie and Mary were staying.

Mam was really unhappy when she found out there wasn't a Catholic church for the children to go to on a Sunday, but as Aunt Molly said, there was a church in a nearby village called Moreton Mill and the Bytheways and Bettons took them there each week.

Pop had to tell Mam off once when she asked if Aunt Molly and Uncle Fred had children. She knew they didn't and Tom sensed it made Aunt Molly in particular upset. He also thought he knew why his mother had said it. It was simply a really difficult time for everyone.

Mam softened a little as the evening went on. She was delighted at how well her children were being fed; indeed, it was the best food she herself had had. Pop made a joke about livestock rustling, and Uncle Fred laughed.

But Tom saw the glance Aunt Molly gave. PC Purslow had been around again, and Tom had overheard the policeman talking to the Bytheways. He had done his usual of not digesting his food so he had to rush back to the outdoor privy. He didn't think anyone knew he was there. It was obvious from the way Uncle Fred talked to the policeman that he didn't like the questions he was being asked.

Tom stayed where he was after PC Purslow left. He couldn't see them, but he could hear Uncle Fred and Aunt Molly talking quietly. He couldn't hear what they were saying but still thought it best that he wait until they went away so they would not know that he had been there.

They seemed to talk quietly for a very long time, and Tom panicked when Ella appeared in the open doorway to the privy. He put his finger to his lips and the dog seemed to understand. She wagged her tail once and walked away.

Tom breathed a sigh of relief – he knew how naughty it was to eavesdrop. It was ages before Fred and Molly left and he was able to sneak out and re-join the football match. The situation didn't sit well with Tom. It all sounded a bit suspicious.

*

But what the boys did like was the poaching. Uncle Fred started taking them all out at dusk, teaching them some tricks of the trade.

None of them really knew what poaching was to start with, and when Uncle Fred told them it was catching wild rabbits and shooting pheasant or ducks or whatever you could find, so that you could take it home and cook it, none of them understood why it was illegal.

Why wouldn't you want people to get their own food, especially if there was a shortage due to the war?

"Because the animal is on someone else's land. Because posh people like Colonel Gwilt and all the other landed gentry want it for themselves," Fred Bytheway said. "It don't matter that they got so much already, or that they don't need any extra food or money. It just matters that they keep control of the working man, tha's what it is. They is always trying to keep the working man down, stop 'im from getting a bigger share of the pie."

"What pie's that, Uncle Fred?" John asked. "Rabbit pie?" Philly Brown, who liked pie, listened carefully.

But Tom rolled his eyes. He had heard his pop on many occasions talking about the class struggle, Socialism and the rich oppressing the poor. He had even had John, Tom and the rest of the Boden children chanting the name of the local Labour candidate at the last general election. Tom remembered it vividly. He must have only been about five, but he loved walking down Scotland Road with thousands of other people singing, "Vote, vote, vote for Davie Logan!" Davie Logan got in, but then there was never going to be any other result.

"It's not a real pie, John," Fred said. "Imagine having a really big bucket full of money. When it comes to giving everyone their share, how much do you think you would get?"

"We never really have any money," John said.

"Exactly. But how much do you think Colonel Gwilt gets out of that bucket? Look at 'is house."

The boys looked to their left where the colonel's house stood on the hill overlooking the village and the fields beyond. It really was a mansion.

"There's only 'im in there. How big is your house back in Liverpool? The point I am making is Colonel Gwilt has far more money than he needs and people like us, people like your mam and pop, and your mother and brother, Philly, don't have very much. So I see it as my civic duty to take a few rabbits for the pot from his land. We've just got to make sure we don't get caught, eh boys?"

Tom smiled. He really did like Uncle Fred. Philly Brown understood what had been said, but John still looked a bit confused. Tom knew he was still wondering where the pie was, but both of them soon had other things on their minds.

Uncle Fred had started to stoop as he approached the hedge that separated the Bytheway farm from Gwilt's land. Ella slunk down as well and crept forward on her belly. The boys knew to be quiet. The colonel had gamekeepers, and it was these that Uncle Fred was wary of. One night he'd shown the boys where one of them had shot him with rock salt when he was poaching with his own dad many years before. You could still see the little scars in his back where the salt crystals had hit him.

"Stung a fair bit," Uncle Fred admitted.

The four of them crawled through a gap in the hedge, with Fred in the lead. He gave a simple hand single and Ella lay still where she was, waiting. The farmer stopped at the edge of the next field and looked around, the boys staying silent and still behind him. Then Fred started moving again and the boys followed.

They hurried across the field towards another hedge. It was the field beyond where Uncle Fred wanted to poach that night. And it was a dangerous business. The four of them waited by the second hedge until their eyes had accustomed to the gloom. They looked out and listened for two things: rabbits and gamekeepers.

When Fred was happy with the situation, the plan would spring into action. He would give Tom a torch he had brought with him and tell him to point it at the rabbit he wanted. On Fred's word, Tom would turn on the torch and keep it pointed at the rabbit, which would be standing still, transfixed by the beam. Fred would aim and shoot, and he never missed. Then he would quickly tell Tom to point the torch at another rabbit and Fred would shoot that one as well.

Once he had fired twice, John and Philly Brown would rush out and grab the dead rabbits before Tom turned off the torch and they all ran off back towards the farm.

Tom had wanted to rush out and get one of the rabbits, but John had said he was too slow and speed was crucial. That's why Philly always ran out as well, leaving Tom with the torch. Sometimes shouting could be heard as they rushed back to the farm, but they never got caught. Ella would jump up at them excitedly and the boys loved it. It was only much later that Tom realised Fred was doing it just to entertain the boys.

"If poaching is taking rabbits off someone else's land, Uncle Fred, and it's against the law, why don't you just shoot the rabbits that are on your land?" he had asked.

"But where's the fun in that?" Fred had replied, smiling.

They often went poaching on Colonel Gwilt's land.

*

But there were chores to be done as well. Uncle Fred made sure the boys helped plenty with the farm's pigs and sheep as well as feeding the ducks and the geese and the chickens. Feeding the birds became Tom's job as Fred laughed at him when he asked what the white birds in the yard actually were.

Even for a city boy, the farmer reckoned, Tom should have known, so Fred gave him feeding responsibility, joking that Tom would soon learn which was which. Tom felt aggrieved. He had only asked a question and suddenly he was stuck with feeding the birds every day. The geese were vicious and more than once chased him around the yard. On one occasion one even flew at him, but he managed to duck down just in time.

But that was nothing compared to what had happened to John when he was feeding the pigs one Saturday. Pop was due to come and visit later, and Fred decided that was what John was thinking about when he got jumped by one of the big boars in the pig field. It came at him from behind, and before John knew what was happening, the huge animal had knocked him to the ground and was trying to bite one of his legs. John screamed, alerting Fred and Philly Brown, who were in the sheep field. Fred ran straight to where John was, Philly trying to keep up. But Ella got there first, barking and growling at the much bigger animal. She tried to nip the boar's ankles. Fred was shouting and screaming as he neared John and kicked hard at the animal's neck as it kept biting the boy's leg. The boar reared away from the kick, giving Fred enough time to grab John and throw him over his shoulder.

"Get out, Philly!" Fred Bytheway shouted as he started to run out of the field. "Lock the gate behind me!" Safely out of the pig field, Fred lay John on the ground. The boy's face was screwed up in pain as Fred started to lift his trouser leg to see what damage had been done. Tom had heard the screams and came running, as did Aunt Molly. Ella sat and watched; even she looked worried.

John's leg was a bloody mess, and Tom was nearly sick, but once the blood had been wiped away with Aunt Molly's apron, they could see there were just a couple of puncture wounds that were bleeding. By the time the leg had been cleaned properly back in the farmhouse, John had stopped screaming. As well as the two puncture wounds, which had stopped bleeding, there were a number of deep scratches where the boar's teeth had scraped.

"Lucky you weren't wearing shorts," Philly Brown said. They all agreed. It would have been far worse as the animal was obviously aggressive.

When Pop arrived later that day, John was lying on the sofa in the Bytheways' living room. Uncle Fred and Aunt Molly had tried to make him as comfortable as possible and had managed to get him some sweets even though Mr Teece wasn't due in his van for another week. They were both really worried when Pop arrived; John was in their care and he had been badly attacked by one of their farm animals. But they needn't have worried. Pop knew an accident when he saw one and having taken a look for himself and seen that his eldest son was actually all right, he thanked the Bytheways for treating him so quickly and especially for getting the sweets. In fact, by tea time, John could almost put all his weight on his injured leg, so it really looked much worse than it was.

"I might even be able to play football tomorrow," John said, but everyone knew he was being too hopeful.

*

Again, Pop left the next day and everyone continued as normal as they could. John's leg soon healed, and he was back on the football field. Work on the farm increased as autumn turned to winter and the weather got colder. One chore the boys shared was fetching water from the outside pump. It hadn't been a problem to start with, although the handle was a bit on the rusty side, so it could take a bit of effort to pump. But once the temperatures dropped, the metal handle got really, really cold.

Once, on a particularly bitter December morning, Philly Brown came back into the farmhouse with tears streaming down his face. He put the pail of water on the floor in the kitchen and held his other hand out to Aunt Molly. It was red raw and bleeding. Philly Brown's skin had stuck to the freezing water pump handle and he had left some of it there when he wrenched his hand away. It was a nasty one, but Philly was brave.

Winter was hard. The snow came one day and sent Fred into a completely different mode. Suddenly the sheep needed feeding by hand because the grass in the fields was frozen and under a foot of snow. Hay that had been collected in the early autumn and stored in the barn was now carried out into the field at the back. The sheep came rushing up to the boys and Fred, snatching the icy dried grass from their hands. By the end of the feed, no one could feel their hands. Once they had washed them and warmed them up, they realised their hands were full of tiny little cuts where the frozen hay had scratched at their skin.

The same thing happened when they changed the straw in the pigsties. Because it was made out of the stalks of wheat and other crops, it was even rougher than the hay and the cuts opened up again. Tom realised that although it was a hard life in Liverpool, when winter came to Shropshire, it was much worse. There was rarely ever any snow in the city, although the winds whipping up off the River Mersey could have you frozen in seconds. But snow on the ground – the freezing blizzards of hail and sleet and the fact that the boys had to be out in it helping Fred to feed the animals – was a completely different type of cold. The boys tried, but at times the winter in Shropshire even put a stop to football games with Ted Edwards.

THE BETTONS' HOUSE

Christmas in High Hatton

It was Christmas Eve and there was snow on the ground.
The boys were excited. So were the girls. Mam and Pop
would be getting a shock when they arrived. It never
seemed to snow much in Liverpool.

Tom was staring out the window. He wanted to go
out, but it was much too cold, so they were all in the
Bytheways' living room. Meg was in her Girl Guide
mode, showing Chrissie and Mary how to create intricate
paper cuttings they were going to use to decorate the
table for Christmas dinner. John and Philly Brown were
helping Aunt Molly make coloured paper chains to hang
from the ceiling. It took their minds off the waiting.
Mam, Pop and Philly Brown's ma were all coming to
stay for Christmas.

Tom couldn't wait, and he certainly couldn't be
bothered with paper chains when he was so desperate to
see his mam and pop. It seemed like ages since they had
last been up – before even the snow, as Pop could no
longer cycle down from Liverpool on a weekend. It was
just too dark and dangerous.

Fred had gone to fetch them from somewhere, but
Tom didn't know how far it was or how long it would
take them coming back in the tractor. Not for the first
time he smiled at the thought of Mam being knocked
about in the trailer as Fred's tractor puffed its way along
the narrow, snow-laden country lanes.

They were really lucky. As far as Tom knew, not all of the other parents could make it down to High Hatton for Christmas, and there were lots of evacuated children in the village really upset that they would spend Christmas alone. But Philly Brown's brother, Robbie, had somehow managed to arrange for an army truck to take their parents somewhere nearby so Fred would be able to pick them up.

Somewhere behind Tom, Mary gasped. Meg had finished cutting up a square piece of paper which she then unfolded to reveal the most beautiful design. It was to go in the middle of the dinner table. With one done, she handed the scissors to Mary and watched carefully as Mary attempted to do her own much smaller one. It was going to be a big dinner and they needed twelve individual cuttings so that everyone had one on the table.

"A bit higher, John," Aunt Molly said as John stood on tiptoe trying to stick one end of the paper chain to the wall.

"I can't. I need a chair," he replied, giving up and waiting as Philly Brown let go of his end of the chain and went to get one from the kitchen.

Tom leapt up from the sofa. He heard Fred's tractor long before he saw it and he rushed out into the lane to watch it arrive. Snow fell steadily, and he blinked a lot when snowflakes landed in his eyes. He thought he could make out the exhaust coming out of the tractor, but against the falling snow and the grey sky, he wasn't sure.

"Get back inside, Tom. You'll catch your death!"

But Tom ignored Molly Bytheway and stayed where he was. It was cold, but he wanted to see Mam and Pop more than anything.

After what seemed like ages, the tractor appeared around the bend in the lane and Tom's heart skipped a beat. He ran towards it and immediately fell over.

The snow in the lane had been packed tight and the fresh snow on top made it incredibly slippery. He dusted himself down, barely noticing the pain in his knee where he had fallen and made his way more carefully.

"Mam!" he yelled when he was close enough. "Pop!"

"Get back inside, our Tom. You'll freeze!" Mam replied, looking like a very uncomfortable snowman in the trailer, because it didn't have a roof and she was covered in white.

Pop just grinned. He was always very cheery and getting thrown about didn't faze him. He was used to hard work and being uncomfortable. He saw the trailer ride as a bit of fun. Mam and Philly Brown's ma didn't.

Tom turned to race back to the farm and fell over again. John, Chrissie, Mary and Philly Brown were all out in the lane now, as was Meg. Philly Brown was making a snowball.

It needed to hit Pop, or Fred, Tom thought as the mothers would not be amused if it hit them. As it was, he missed completely.

Fred turned the tractor into the driveway and the children gathered round the back of the trailer, desperate to cuddle their parents.

Molly Bytheway stood by her front door, which was closed to keep the heat in. She was beaming. She had grown very fond of all of the children and was so happy to see them fussing as Pop and Fred helped the mothers off the back of the trailer.

"Inside!" Mam said as her children hung onto her coattails. "It's far too cold."

Philly Brown's ma shook hands with Molly Bytheway, who had opened the front door to let everyone in.

She hadn't made it down to Shropshire once since the children had been evacuated. It showed as Philly Brown was stuck to her – he'd missed his mother so much that he wouldn't let her go.

"Oh, how lovely!" Margie Brown said as she entered the living room. "And so warm."

Fred took her coat, and Pop plonked a large sack by the Christmas tree the children had decorated the week before.

"They our presents, Pop?" John said.

"They might be," Pop laughed, giving his eldest a playful cuff around the ear. "You'll just have to wait and see. I've yet to speak to Father Christmas, so I don't know if you've all been good enough for presents."

Mary's face fell.

"He's only kidding," Chrissie said, giving her sister a comforting pat. "Aren't you, Pop?" she asked, suddenly a bit nervous herself.

"Course! Now come here and give your old Pop a big cuddle. I've missed you all so much."

Fred had taken Mam's coat as well and the two Liverpool women sat themselves down on the sofa, the Boden children fussing about them and Philly Brown sitting on his mother's knee, even though he was a bit big to be doing such things. The children were all talking at once while Pop, Fred and Molly looked on, happy to see them so excited.

"I'll get the kettle on," Molly Bytheway said, busying herself. She was the only one in the room who was a little sad. Seeing the children so happy made her once again lament the fact that she didn't have any of her own.

"Well said, Molly love," her husband said. "It's freezing out there. I think we all need to warm up a bit."

—

84

The adults settled down to their cups of tea. Mugs of milk for the children, except Meg, who liked tea and secretly thought it made her look more grown up.

Shortly after the Liverpool parents had arrived, her mum and dad had also come round, so the Bytheways had a really full house. The women crowded onto the sofa while the men sat at the table.

"It's that bloody Alfie Donoghue that's done it," Mam was saying.

"He's a good lad, Saranne," Pop said. "He'll do right by our Sarah."

"That's true enough," Philly Brown's ma chipped in. "You've nothing to worry about with that lad. He's a good 'un, all right."

"I know," Mam said. "But there are so many gossips on Conyers Street, she'll have to come in the back way when she starts to show. And I've no idea what Father Peter is going to make of it all."

"Ach! That old busybody. He can take his old-fashioned views and stick them where the sun doesn't shine!" Molly Bytheway and Lily Betton laughed, but they knew that as Catholics, the Bodens took the news that their eldest daughter, Sarah, was pregnant very seriously.

It wouldn't be a problem in High Hatton – at least not amongst most people. They might live in the middle of nowhere, but there wasn't the same stigma about being pregnant out of wedlock as there clearly was in Liverpool.

"He'll be marrying her soon enough," Philly Brown's ma added, still trying to cheer Mam Boden up.

"And I'm not sure we've got the room. When this war's over and they all come back, it will be three or four to a bed for the boys. I don't know what we'll do."

"We'll manage fine, love," Pop said. "And they'll get their own house soon enough."

Mam Boden dabbed a tear from her eye. Philly Brown's ma patted her on the leg. Molly Bytheway and Lily Betton looked on, concerned. The poor woman was clearly very worried.

Pop, Fred Bytheway and Alf Betton talked about the war. All thoughts of it ending by Christmas had long since been forgotten. Poland had been divided up between Germany and the Soviet Union and the Russians were busy fighting in Finland.

"Overwhelming odds, them," said Pop. "I'm not sure how much longer the Finns can hold out."

"But they've got winter on their side, Jack," Alf Betton added. "Can't be easy for the Russians fighting in all that snow."

"Maybe, but the Russians have enough snow of their own," Fred Bytheway put in. The three men nodded in agreement. "Do you think our army can do anything to stop Hitler?" he asked.

Nobody knew. It was obvious they were being told things by the government that weren't the whole truth. The whole truth never came out in wartime. But the British had been building up its army for over a year now and had troops stationed in Belgium.

"Our Matty's out there," Pop said.

"So's my brother," Alf Betton replied. "I worry about him every day. From what I hear we've got good defences, but the way the Germans went through Poland, and the agreement they've got with the Soviets, Hitler's got all those troops. It's going to be very bloody."

Tom hung on every word. The war had worried him terribly from the moment it had been declared. He knew it was really serious and that it would hurt families everywhere.

As well as his Uncle Matty, Philly Brown's older brother Robbie was at sea as a DEMS gunner. As exciting as it sounded, he wasn't sure he fancied being on deck if a German U-boat fired its torpedoes.

The rest of the children had gone outside. The novelty of seeing their parents had worn off as soon as the adults started talking about grown-up things. Only Tom liked to stay and listen, but then there were shouts from outside and Tom soon changed his mind and went to join his friends.

They had built a snowman, or at least half of one, but it had turned into a full-on snowball fight. There were sounds of others playing nearby as well; Ted Edwards was in the football field with his mates. They had been busy and had built two massive snowmen that put the Conyers Street Gang's effort to shame.

"Ambush!" John screamed as they all piled through the gate and attacked Ted's lot with snowballs. Philly Brown got a bit excited and jumped on Ted, hurting the bigger boy.

It looked like they were going to have a fight, but John calmed things down with a well-aimed snowball that got Philly right in the back of his head.

They had all become really great friends over the last few months. They'd played endless games of football and, more often than not, got up to mischief in Meg's woods. Rickers and his cronies kept appearing, trying to annoy the younger boys, but they got used to it and it didn't bother them.

As soon as they appeared, someone grabbed the ball and made sure the bigger boys couldn't get it. It sometimes turned into a bit of piggy-in-the-middle as they threw the ball around.

It often meant Rickers would try to start a fight, but despite being a few years older, they were always outnumbered and got as good as they gave.

Rickers was stupid, but his mates were worse. It was the only reason Tom could think of as to why they kept coming back, even though the younger boys were no longer scared of them and they never got the ball anymore.

Of course, if they found you on your own, that was a different matter – as Tom and a few of the others had found to their cost.

*

When they got back inside, it was as if nothing had changed. All the adults were in exactly the same position as they had been before. The men were still talking about the war, but the women had moved on to rationing. Mam and Philly Brown's ma were really struggling, they said, and couldn't believe how easy it was for Molly Bytheway and Lily Betton to get food on the table out in the countryside as they were.

But both were really pleased with how well their children looked. It was probably the best food they had ever had, and Mam in particular was grateful for that. She realised she'd been a bit off the first time she visited but had got more used to someone else looking after her children and was pleased the Bytheways seemed such decent people.

"Are we going to do Midnight Mass?" Mam asked later as she went into the kitchen with Molly Bytheway.

Tom and John heard this and looked at each other. There was nothing worse for them.

"Not a chance, I'm afraid, Saranne," Fred Bytheway chimed. "That snow's not letting up – it would be madness to go out in it. The church is just too far."

"Don't worry, though. They've been to church every Sunday, just like you asked," Molly Bytheway added.

And it was true. The boys didn't mind this as much. The church services they were going to now seemed shorter and much less serious. Back home, Father Peter could talk for hours, and often did.

"John, Tom, Philly Brown, outside," Fred Bytheway said. "I've something to show you. You too if you like, Jack."

Pop knew what Fred was up to and wanted to see for himself. The five of them filed out of the back door into the freezing cold. Fred took them across the yard and into the barn where the ducks and geese were housed.

"Okay, boys, pick one."

John, Tom and Philly Brown looked round, unsure what Uncle Fred had meant.

"Don't just stand there – we need one for the pot tomorrow." Pop and Fred were smiling, as was Alf Betton who had also joined them. Ella was there too, panting away.

Pop wanted to see how his sons would react, but it was Philly Brown who moved first. The birds went mad as he waded into the middle of them.

"Pick a big one, Philly Brown, we've a lot of mouths to feed." The noise was deafening in the barn. It reminded Tom of Colonel Gwilt's shrieking violin a bit. Philly Brown had cornered a group of the birds, each of them looking at him warily and honking and quacking their alarm.

He dived right into the middle of them all and missed.

John and Tom laughed, then John waded in as well. In no time he had a big goose under his arm and was holding its neck so it couldn't peck at him. Philly Brown had also caught one by then and held his aloft like a trophy.

"Fair enough – we'll have two," Fred said. "We'll take them next door. We don't want the others to see what we're about to do."

In the other barn, where the winter feed for the pigs and sheep was kept, Fred Bytheway positioned a stool. "Come on then, Tom, your turn to hold your Christmas dinner."

Pop kept smiling. He'd seen nothing like it in Liverpool and was very proud that his sons seemed to have taken to the rural life so easily.

"I'll show you how it's done," Fred said. "And you can do the next one."

Tom eyed him nervously. He knew animals had to be slaughtered and that they didn't just miraculously turn into sausages or bacon, but he had never killed one himself. Fred Bytheway took John's bird from him and sat himself down on the stool.

"Right, first you puts the body of the bird between your legs and squeeze just a little so it don't fly off." Everyone was enthralled as the farmer expertly managed the massive white bird and placed it exactly as he said. "Then you stretch its neck up and twist it slightly to one side. When you've got him like that, you takes your knife and you pushes it in just behind the ear, then twist."

With one swift push and flick the bird slumped.

"Blimey, that was quick," Pop said, admiring Fred's handiwork. "Bet he didn't feel a thing. Reckon you can do that, our Tom?" Tom wasn't sure. But he felt as though he was under pressure to do it, so he said he could.

"Come on, then," Fred said, still holding the now dead bird by its neck. "Get yerself comfortable on 'ere. Philly Brown bring yours over."

"Can I not do it?" Philly Brown asked.

"You and John caught them, so I reckon young Tom here needs to do his bit. Can't be getting a free lunch, can he?"

"Go on, Tom," Pop said to his younger son. "Make a man of you, that will."

It gave Tom a bit of confidence, but also more pressure. He really had to do it now and he didn't want anyone laughing at him. He sat down. Fred took the bird from Philly Brown and squatted down next to Tom. The bird suddenly seemed even bigger.

"There we are. Body between the legs. Not too tight. Now stretch the neck a little."

Tom was really nervous but did exactly as he was told. Fred handed him the knife and helped Tom position it.

"In and twist. That's all it needs."

Tom took a deep breath, closed his eyes and pushed the knife in.

"And twist," Fred said once more. Tom did, and he felt the bird go limp. He opened his eyes. The bird was dead, and it hadn't even honked. It had been easy.

"Right," said Fred. "Now to pluck 'em."

The boys spent what seemed like hours pulling off the feathers and stuffing them into a sack. The excitement of the slaughter soon faded and even Ella got bored watching, sloping off back to her kennel to sleep. The boys' hands started to ache with the constant grabbing and pulling out of feathers. It was just another farming job the boys had not done before.

Two of them would pluck and the third would stuff the feathers in a sack. Nothing seemed to get wasted out in the countryside. Fred had said they'd be used in pillows, as he and Pop left the boys to it in the barn. By the time they'd finished, their hands were in agony and they were all freezing.

"Yeah, but they'll be nice to eat tomorrow," Philly Brown said as they crossed the yard back to the farmhouse, the birds now naked, pink and a little scrawny looking. They certainly did not look as magnificent as they had when they were alive.

"Good lads," Fred called through when he heard the boys open the back door. "Stick 'em on the kitchen table and Molly'll get cracking in the morning."

The boys were exhausted and they all collapsed by the fire to get warm. Meg, Chrissie and Mary had finished the paper table decorations and were creating a last paper chain, which Uncle Fred stuck to the ceiling – him being so much taller than Pop.

The women still sat on the sofa and laughed away, sipping at their sherry. All except Mam, who had asked if she could have a milk stout instead. Molly Bytheway had been a bit surprised by the request. The men were drinking ale out of impressive-looking tankards. Uncle Fred's was made out of metal.

It was all Tom could do to keep his eyes open as the heat washed over him and his aching hands got the feeling back into them. It wasn't long before John and Philly Brown got bored and went and sat next to the men, glasses of milk at their elbows.

Tom stayed where he was but listened as he always did.

Would the Americans join in? What about the Japanese? And which side would they be on? They'd been fighting the Chinese for years now and there was real concern they might start to target some of Britain's empire in the Far East. The war that was meant to be over by now was getting very serious indeed, and no one could quite believe that it was openly discussed as a potential second world war.

Tom's eyelids drooped a final time and he nodded off.

*

Tom opened his eyes but could see nothing in the pitch dark. But he could hear Pop snoring next to him and he could tell Mam was asleep on his other side. He had no memory of going to bed.

He raised his head a little and thought he could make out John and Philly Brown asleep in the single bed.

"All right, our kid? Merry Christmas!"

Oh my God, thought Tom. It was Christmas Day!

"Merry Christmas to you, Pop," he said back. Just a tiny move had been enough to wake up his dad. "What time is it?"

"Early, lad. You were out for the count last night. Country air, eh? Get your head down for a bit longer. Big day today."

But Tom couldn't get back to sleep. How could he? It was Christmas Day and there were presents to be had. He lay as still as he could so as to not wake anyone else up. He lay there for ages imagining what presents he might be getting from the sack Pop had brought with him. Mam stirred, and he tried doubly hard not to move. When he heard the sounds of someone walking around downstairs he decided it was okay to get up.

Pop groaned as he clambered over the top of him, then found his slippers in the dark and put them on. It was Aunt Molly who was up, and she was already busy in the kitchen, putting one of the geese in the oven.

"Morning, Sleepy Joe. Glass of milk?" It was poured before Tom had a chance to answer. "Fred must've really worked you yesterday. You fell asleep right in front of the fire and didn't even wake up when you were carried upstairs."

"I know. I don't remember going up."

"Your dad carried you. How about you give me some help and peel those spuds? This is going to be a very big dinner with all your parents and the Bettons coming."

Tom's heart sank as he saw the huge pile of potatoes, and his right hand ached after all that feather plucking the night before.

But the Bytheways were really good people and he was always happy to help out on the farm. He picked up a knife and the first potato.

It wasn't long before there was a thundering of feet and John and Philly Brown burst into the kitchen as well. Aunt Molly had already poured them some milk.

"Christmas Day, our Tom!" John said before eagerly gulping down his drink. "Presents!" he said, wiping the white moustache from his upper lip.

Uncle Fred came down next, then Mam and Pop, Mam busying herself helping Aunt Molly and taking over the spud peeling, which Tom was making a mess of.

Pop sat in the living room with the boys and to pass the time told them of his adventures in the Navy. He'd been shipwrecked loads of times and on one occasion he struggled ashore with a mate.

It had been pitch dark, but they saw a light on in a house and made their way over. It was in southern Ireland, and the man who opened the door didn't like the English, but he let them in once Pop told him he had Irish parents.

The man had even heard of the Scotland Road area in Liverpool, where all the Irish immigrants, such as the Bodens, tended to live.

When Pop and his friend were allowed in to get dry and warm by the fire, they found the family had four goats in there with them. They were their livelihood.

One of the goats tried to eat Pop's trousers and bit him. The boys always laughed at that bit, but this morning, Christmas morning, they struggled to keep their attention off the presents lying under the tree.

Pop must've got them out the night before, Tom thought, because they were no longer in the sack he had brought them in.

They weren't allowed to even touch them until the girls came, not that that stopped John, who had a sneaky feel of his when Pop wasn't looking.

Tom was almost bursting, and it seemed to take forever before the Bettons turned up with Chrissie, Mary and Meg as well as Philly Brown's ma, who had stayed with them.

"Come on, then. Let's get it over with," Pop said. Everyone had crowded into the living room and the children jostled each other as they sat around the tree. Each of them was given an orange, something they always got at Christmas because they were such a treat, but it was the presents the children were really after.

"Youngest first," said Pop, handing a small parcel to Mary. They were all quite small parcels, except Chrissie's and Philly Brown's.

Mary squealed with delight when she unwrapped hers. It was a skipping rope with beautiful wooden handles. She jumped up and gave Pop a huge cuddle, then ran to Mam and did the same.

Chrissie was busy unwrapping her parcel. Tom was trying to work out when it would be his turn. Was he before or after Meg? He was younger than Philly Brown by a few months.

"I love it!" Chrissie beamed as she found she had been given a doll. It came in a box that made the parcel larger.

"We thought it looked like you, love," Mam said, as Chrissie stared wide-eyed at the little ginger-haired doll with pale-coloured skin. She also gave her mam a cuddle.

"Meg," said Alf Betton, handing his daughter her present. It was in coloured paper, with pictures of Father Christmas all over it. The Bodens' presents were in plain brown paper. Meg gasped. It was a pocket knife and the boys were instantly jealous. She started pulling out all the different blades and tools.

"Careful; it's sharp," Alf Betton said as Meg ran her finger along the largest blade. "One of them Swiss Army things," he added. She was speechless and already thinking about what she was going to do with it. A sharpened stick for spearing fish in her river? Wood carving? Chopping down trees?

"Tom, your turn." Tom daren't open his parcel. Everyone had had brilliant ones so far. What if he didn't like his? It was quite heavy and long and thin. As he started peeling away the paper he caught a glimpse of something silver and shiny. Then he pulled it out.

"A torch! That's brilliant!" He looked up at his pop, instantly grateful and delighted at the same time.

"It's magic, you know? It shines in different colours. And it's got batteries in it." Tom looked more closely at the head end of the torch and could see it was grooved. Tom fiddled then twisted the body and noticed a red filter slide over the bulb. He switched it on. Red light flooded out. He twisted the end again; blue, then green, then clear. He couldn't believe what he had been given and jumped up to give Mam a huge hug. The adults looked on happily. The children were so pleased with their presents.

"Here you are, our Philly," Philly Brown's ma said as she handed him a huge plain white parcel.

"Ta, Ma!" he replied, ripping the paper to shreds to reveal a Meccano set. John whistled. Philly Brown just stared at the box. Two little boys were pictured building what looked like a crane out of green and red metal pieces. He couldn't believe his eyes as he held in his hands something he had always wanted.

"Bloke that invented that came from Liverpool, you know," Pop said. "Died a few years back."

"Frank Hornby?" Alf Betton asked as Philly Brown squeezed his ma, holding the box under one arm. Pop nodded.

"And now you, our John."

John's had been the smallest parcel. He tore off the paper and looked blankly at the thing he held. It had silver sides, but wood in the middle where there were a series of holes. He looked up at Pop, who was smiling.

"It's a mouth organ, son."

"A what?"

"Blow in it. It's a musical instrument."

John blew. Nothing happened.

"Here," said Fred Bytheway, taking the organ from John. "You don't just blow, you sort of suck, I think."

He put the instrument to his mouth and managed a couple of squeaks.

"Well done," said Alf Betton, laughing. "I think you've broken it, Fred!"

Fred Bytheway had another go, only this time he managed to get a few notes together. It wasn't a nice sound; he clearly needed practice. He handed it back to John, who had another go and managed a squeak of his own.

"There you go, son. You'll be blaring it out like Charlie Parker soon." Pop loved a bit of Jazz.

*

Christmas Day flew by in a blur. Tom went up to the bedroom and closed the curtains so he could shine his magic torch about. John, already, was getting quite good with his mouth organ.

They had all had a go and struggled the first time they tried but got sound later. All except Mary, who simply could not get a note out of it and was convinced it really was broken.

Meg spent the day cutting things up with her new knife, and she had joined the boys when Philly Brown started building his Meccano set. Outside in the yard, Mam and Philly Brown's ma held the skipping rope as Mary and Chrissie jumped.

Christmas dinner was huge. Lily Betton had been cooking at her own house and Alf and Uncle Fred brought the food over when it was ready. She had cooked the other goose and loads of vegetables. There was even a massive pot for all the gravy they needed.

Aunt Molly brought out a Christmas ham as well as loads of pigs in blankets. Those were Tom's favourite. And Philly Brown's. They must have each eaten hundreds.

They weren't so keen on the sprouts, but Pop had their share. Tom noticed the Bytheways exchange a glance when Mam Boden asked them where they got all the food from.

Alf Betton jumped in and said it was because they lived in the country and you could always get food if you knew where to look. Pop changed the subject; he had seen it made their hosts a little uncomfortable, not that his wife had been implying anything.

Afterwards, the grown-ups fell asleep in the living room. The children were still too excited. Once changed out of their pyjamas, they played with their new toys.

John had been told to play in the barn so the adults could nod off in peace. He stopped playing when the sounds of football came from the field. It was tricky in the snow, but they still tried.

Tom played, but Philly Brown was fascinated by his Meccano and stayed in to play with it all day. Meg was off somewhere with her knife and Chrissie and Mary fussed over Chrissie's new doll.

They were all back in when it got dark and the adults woke up from their afternoon naps. They had listened to the king as he gave his Christmas address over the wireless. There were lots of thoughtful nods as the king talked about the tragedy of the war.

There was also loads of food left over and everyone picked at it as the night wore on. John really was getting quite good at his mouth organ and even played a few bars of a song to everyone.

He had worked out that you got different notes if you both blew and sucked, so you could continue playing without stopping for breath. Chrissie had joined in, humming away, and the two of them were really quite good together. "A double act!" as Pop had said.

As the night wore on, the children grew tired. When Mary fell asleep, Mam and Pop decided it was time for the girls to head back to the Bettons' house. Alf stayed behind to talk to Pop and Fred, but Philly Brown's ma went with Lily Betton.

Philly Brown was very quiet as he watched them leave. His ma was leaving for Liverpool in the morning along with the Bodens. It had been a great day and he'd been so pleased to see her, but he realised it was nearly over. It had been too quick.

The boys went up together a bit later, leaving the grown-ups to talk downstairs. They were tired but fighting against it. Tom had his torch and they all played with it, trying to create shadow shapes on the wall of their bedroom.

They managed a rabbit shape by holding up two fingers, but not much else. They squeezed into the single bed, leaving the double for Mam and Pop, and shined the torch on the ceiling. John and Philly Brown were soon asleep, and Mam and Pop came up together soon after.

But Tom was wide awake and still holding his torch. Red was the best colour for inside the now dark room as it didn't wake anyone up. He imagined he was working on an anti-aircraft gun, looking out for German bombers.

There was a noise of a door opening and closing. Curious, he got up and went to the window, opening it carefully so he could shine his magic torch outside. The cold air rushed in and made Tom shiver. But he saw someone walking off down the lane. Tom checked the torch was on its red filter and pointed it at the figure. He turned the torch off quickly.

What was Uncle Fred doing out at this time of night?

THE FOOTBALL FIELD

The Boys Go Out at Night

Tom woke up to find the bedroom was empty. John and Philly Brown must have gone downstairs with Mam and Pop, he thought as he got dressed and hurried down. He was annoyed with himself. His parents were leaving that morning, but his night-time discovery had left him lying in bed thinking for a long time after about Uncle Fred's mysterious late-night walk.

Tom didn't hear him come back, so he now thought Uncle Fred must have been gone for some time. He was back now, though, in the kitchen talking to Pop about war as everyone ate leftovers for breakfast, washed down with glasses of milk and mugs of tea.

"All right, Tom, lad?" Fred Bytheway said as he saw him in the doorway.

"Here he is," Pop added. "You sure do like your kip out here in the countryside, don't you, our Tom?"

"Sorry, Pop," he said, feeling awkward with everyone's eyes on him. "When are you leaving?"

"Not for a couple of hours yet," Mam said. "The girls are due soon; then your uncle Fred's taking us back in that tractor thing of his." Fred laughed. He knew the women had hated being cooped up in his trailer being snowed on. It was not a comfortable experience for them. But the snow had stopped since then and the roads looked much more passable. At least they wouldn't all look like snowmen this time.

Chrissie burst in through the backdoor, closely followed by Mary and Meg. She was still clutching her doll; she adored it. And Mary had her skipping rope in her hand. There would be much more skipping later.

Lily and Alf Betton walked in with Philly Brown's ma a short time later, and the noise level in the kitchen rose again as everyone started chatting to each other.

Tom made his way round to John, keeping a wary eye on Fred Bytheway. "I've got something to tell you later," he whispered. John knew an important secret when he heard one. He trusted Tom's instincts as his second-in-command of the Conyers Street Gang.

The two walked away from each other so as not to look suspicious. But Pop had seen them. He would have a word with them before he left as he didn't want his boys getting into trouble like they always seemed to manage.

The morning passed quickly. It felt like no time before Fred Bytheway had fired up the tractor and Pop was helping Mam and Philly Brown's ma into the trailer. It was very emotional for all of them, but both the children and the grown-ups had had the best Christmas they could remember.

Mam in particular was itching to get back to Liverpool and have a second Christmas with her other children. They had left the younger ones under the control of Sarah, Winnie and Kitty and knew that everything would be all right.

Pop came over to John and Tom. "I saw you two whispering," he said, quietly. "No funny business, you hear? Or you'll have me to answer to." Then he gave each of them a clip round the ear before hugging them and nearly squeezing the life out of them.

Tom was appalled that Pop had seen them. He had been so careful. John just looked blank, as if he had no idea what Pop was talking about. Pop smiled. His eldest boy was good at pretending, and he admired him for it.

And that was that. Christmas was over. They realised they wouldn't see their parents again for a long time. There were tears and blown kisses and even Aunt Molly had to dry her eyes. Pop looked as cheery as he could and comforted the women in the trailer as it bounded down the road and out of sight.

"Fred's got a bit of feeding to do today, boys." Alf Betton said. "He's asked me to supervise." John groaned, but Tom had grown to quite like feeding time. He was used to the geese and ducks, and feeding them wasn't as hard on the hands as giving frozen straw to the pigs or frozen hay to the sheep. Philly didn't mind doing anything. He was always smiling.

"And girls," Molly Bytheway added, "you're helping me clear up after yesterday. The house is like a bombsite!" Mary wasn't happy, but Chrissie beamed. She always liked helping. Her doll, and skipping, could wait.

*

After they had done their chores for the day, John and Tom went looking for Ted Edwards to see if his lot wanted to play football. They found them soon enough in the centre of the village having a huge snowball fight.

There must have been about thirty of them and they threw snowballs until their hands were raw. They were soaked through as well and got really muddy when they finally played a game of football. For a change Meg wasn't there and neither was Philly Brown, who had decided to stay in the farmhouse building his Meccano set.

Tom had been through on goal at one point, something that almost never happened, and he smashed the ball with all his strength. It sailed high and wide. Ted Edwards stood by the penalty spot, hands on hips and looking very unimpressed. He had been in a much better position. Tom saw the look and felt sheepish. "I'll fetch," he offered, but he felt his cheeks getting even redder than they already were from the running about and the cold wind.

In the distance they heard Fred Bytheway's tractor crawling along the lane. It jolted Tom's memory and he told his brother about what he had seen the night before.

"We'll have to tell Philly Brown as well," John said, but Tom wasn't so sure. He was great, was Philly, but Tom felt nervous that he was accusing their guardian of being up to something. "He might have some ideas himself," John added. "I think we need to tell him." Tom reluctantly agreed and, complaining that they were freezing, John and Tom headed back to the farmhouse, getting there just as Uncle Fred turned his tractor into the yard.

"Did they get off okay?" John asked.

"Sure did!" Uncle Fred replied. "Fed the animals?" John and Tom nodded. "Good. That's one less thing to worry about!" He looked very happy and went into the kitchen as the boys stood and watched. Tom realised that he was questioning everything that Uncle Fred said, and he didn't like himself for it.

They followed him into the house and Aunt Molly made them strip in the kitchen. She wasn't having mud traipsed all through her house. The boys went upstairs and put on some clean clothes. "And don't you be thinking about going out again – I'm not doing a wash for a few days – you haven't got many clean clothes left."

Dressed, but with muddy hands and faces, John and Tom found Philly Brown working hard at his Meccano set. It looked brilliant, and the crane was really taking shape.

When he was told there was to be a secret gang meeting, Philly Brown stopped immediately and the three of them went outside.

"Where are you going?" Aunt Molly asked. "I told you to keep those clothes clean."

"Just out to the barn, Aunt Molly," John replied. "We won't get muddy."

Inside the barn, Philly Brown sat on a bale. He could feel individual bits of straw digging into him. John looked serious. He often did. And Tom looked worried as he often did.

"Well?" Philly Brown said.

John looked at Tom. "Our Tom saw something last night." Philly Brown looked at Tom, who kicked out at some straw on the floor.

"This is top secret, Philly," John continued. "Not a word to anyone."

Philly Brown nodded. It was clearly serious.

"After we all went to bed last night, I couldn't sleep so I was playing with my torch. I heard the front door go and when I looked out the window, I saw Uncle Fred going out.

"It must have been midnight, or later. He turned right and went off towards that other farm. I turned my torch off and leaped back from the window, so he couldn't see me. I don't think he did – I had it on the red filter and that makes it more difficult to see."

"We know all that, our Tom," John said. "What are you trying to say?"

"Well," Tom said nervously, "you know all this pig rustling business and how we've always got loads of food and that? Well, I think Uncle Fred might be in on it, else why would he be going out so late? And on a really cold night too?"

John and Philly Brown looked at each other. Uncle Fred had been nothing but good to them all, and the Bytheways and Bettons had been brilliant in putting their parents up for Christmas.

"Look," said Tom, pushing his point. "Did you see how they reacted when Mam asked about where they got all the food? Pop changed the subject, but I saw Uncle Fred and Aunt Molly look at each other. There's something going on; I'm sure of it."

"But is that all you have, our Tom?" John said.

Tom thought for a minute. "Well, it's true. There is always loads of food."

"But we live on a farm, Tom," Philly Brown put in. "We have pigs and sheep."

"Yeah," Tom agreed, "but we still seem to have as many as when we first got here. Our animals aren't going missing. It's the ones on Hoggins' farm. And have you seen how often PC Purslow comes round? Whenever there's a pig gone missing, he's round here asking questions. Do you think he suspects Uncle Fred?"

"There wasn't a pig rustled last night. We would have heard about it," John argued.

"Maybe even criminals have Christmas Day off," Tom persisted. "It doesn't explain why he was out so late."

John and Philly Brown could see Tom had a point. He usually did when he had been thinking.

"So what are we going to do about it?" Philly Brown asked.

"I think we need to watch Uncle Fred and see if he goes out again tonight," Tom said. "We could even follow him and see where he goes."

Philly Brown whistled. Things had just got much more intense. "Why don't we just ask Meg?" he said.

"No!" Tom almost shouted. "She's from round here. She's known Uncle Fred and Aunt Molly forever, and her mum and dad are their best friends. Remember how she was when we accused her of stealing our rations? What do you think she'll do if we tell her this?"

Philly Brown looked at the floor. He'd forgotten that it was actually him who had stolen the Bodens' pillowcases of emergency rations and he still felt really bad about it when he remembered.

"We can't say a word to her. Or to Chrissie and Mary as they are really good friends with her. Mary would probably tell her straight away."

John didn't like it one bit. There were five in the Conyers Street Gang, six with Meg as an honorary member. It didn't feel right making plans without telling them. They might need Mary to get through a small gap or something. And they might need Meg's help because she had lived in High Hatton all her life and her local knowledge could be vital in any military operation the gang undertook.

"Agreed," John said. "These could be hardened criminals. We don't want the girls getting hurt."

"Getting hurt how?" Meg Betton said, standing in the doorway to the barn. John and Tom spun around, Tom nearly having a heart attack.

"Nothing," John said quickly.

"No. Out with it." Meg looked scary as she stood in the open doorway, hands on hips, and with her long red hair blowing about in the wind. Nobody said anything.

"Oh, come on! What's the matter with you? How might we girls get hurt?"

"Okay, we'll tell you," John said, raising a hand as Tom was about to protest. "But this is top secret and you cannot tell anyone." Meg nodded and John closed the barn door behind her. "I mean it. This is serious and Tom's usually right about these sorts of things. You need to promise you won't tell."

"I won't," Meg said, getting more annoyed. Tom told her what he had told the boys. The boys looked at her intently. Would she go mad like she had when she was accused of stealing their evacuation rations?

"You're being stupid," she said flatly. "Fred is not in on the pig rustling. No way. He's a farmer and he just wouldn't do that."

"Then how do you explain it? Your dad said it was just country ways that you have loads of food, but something doesn't add up." As always, Tom got upset when someone questioned his thinking. He always got defensive. He knew he was doing it, not really asking for Meg to prove he was wrong, more to prove he was right and that Uncle Fred was indeed a pig rustler. He didn't like himself when he was like that, as if being right was more important than Fred Bytheway being innocent.

"It could be anything. Maybe he was out checking something on his land?" Meg said.

"But he went down the road," Tom said.

"Then maybe he just likes going for walks late at night?" Meg argued. "But you cannot just accuse him like you did with me, remember?" She looked at Philly Brown, who looked away. The four of them stayed silent for a few seconds. It felt a lot longer to Tom, who didn't know what to say anymore.

"Could be a fancy woman?" Philly Brown said.

"What's one of them?" John asked.

"Dunno, but me ma says that Mr McCloskey in Number Eight has one. And he's always going out at strange times."

John and Tom were thoughtful. Most of the people on Conyers Street were great, but one or two were a bit scary. Mr McCloskey was one of them. He never really talked to the kids and didn't seem to have many friends amongst the adults.

"Tea!" Aunt Molly shouted from the back door. It had got dark, but the boys didn't realise how late it actually was.

"Not a word," John said to all of them but mostly to Meg.

"And not a word from you either, John," she answered, pointing a scary-looking finger. "They're good people and they've been really good to you. You're wrong about this, Tom Boden," she added as she left the barn to go back to her house.

The boys were left in silence. John thought Meg was really impressive, like she could be a teacher or a politician or something. Tom was angry. He was sure he was onto something. Philly Brown just thought she was great and terrifying at the same time.

"We need more evidence, then," Tom said. "We'll watch out for him tonight." John and Philly Brown agreed. Tom was usually right. The Conyers Street Gang had a mystery to solve.

*

After their tea the boys busied themselves with Philly Brown's Meccano kit. It looked like they might even have had it finished soon, but then they kept finding they'd gone slightly wrong somewhere.

John took himself off and played with his mouth organ. Tom thought it amazing that he had got so good so quickly.

The Bytheways appreciated the live music in the house and often stopped to listen to it in between their conversations. Tom, in turn, was listening intently to the adults, trying to get any evidence about what was going on, but they said nothing that seemed important and he soon found himself lost in the Meccano set. He had deliberately not brought his magic torch down, though, as he was worried the batteries might run out, and that would be a disaster.

Tom kept an eye on the clock on the mantelpiece. They usually went to bed about ten o'clock, which was later than they did in Liverpool, but they were used to it now. With a knowing wink, Tom pointed to where his watch would have been had he had one; John got the message. The boys had agreed to go up together as soon as it hit ten. It would make them look like they were being good, but really they wanted to make sure they went up as early as possible so they could wait by the window in case Uncle Fred did go out again.

John and Tom were in the double bed again and Philly Brown had the single as they listened out for any sign of anyone going out. They had not put their pyjamas on, however. They wanted to be in outdoor clothes if they were going to follow Uncle Fred in the middle of the night in winter. Eventually, two sets of footsteps came up the stairs and the boys heard Fred and Molly Bytheway talking quietly as if not to wake the boys. Their hearts were almost bursting from their chests. Tom was really nervous, but he was determined to find out what had gone on. Meg's words had hurt him. He didn't like being wrong, but more he didn't like being told, and she really had told him.

———

Soon there was silence. The Bytheways must have gone to sleep as well. Tom was fighting to stay alert, but John and Philly Brown had already nodded off. He could hear them both, breathing quietly in and out. And then, a click. Tom's eyes stretched wide as he heard footsteps going back down the stairs. He shook John awake, holding his hand over his brother's mouth.

"Shhh," he whispered. "Someone's up." The brothers lay there listening for any other noise, but they heard none. Tom got up and tiptoed to the window. It was a clear night. And Fred Bytheway was marching down the lane towards the Hoggins' farm.

"It's him! Quick, get Philly Brown."

In no time the boys had crept downstairs and tried to open the front door. But it had been bolted. Uncle Fred must have gone out the back way. Quiet as they could they went through the kitchen and lifted the latch, running out into the freezing night, trying not to slip. John headed straight up towards the road, as did Philly Brown, and took a careful look around the side of the hedge to see if he could see Uncle Fred in the lane. Tom ran towards Ella to stop the dog from barking. She didn't.

"He's not there!" John said. "Hurry, we need to catch up with him." The boys set off as fast as they could to get to the bend in the road where they needed to stop and look again. Tom got there last as John looked around the edge of the giant oak tree that stood there. At first he couldn't make anything out on the lane, but then a movement caught his eye. A head was bobbing up and down along the driveway to Colonel Gwilt's mansion. It had to be Uncle Fred.

"He's going to Gwilt's?" Tom said, aghast. "But he's meant to be going to Hoggins' farm."

"So are we going to follow him?" Philly Brown asked.

"Of course," said John, "but we need to be careful. He can't see us."

The boys ran along the lane, but not as quickly as before. They were trying to be quiet and hoped Uncle Fred would not hear their heavy breathing or the crunching of snow under their feet. In the silence of the winter's night, their own movement sounded deafening. They stopped again at the entrance to Colonel Gwilt's driveway but could see nothing ahead, so started up the long slope towards the mansion. The house loomed huge out of the darkness as they approached, but they could see a chink of light coming from one of the downstairs windows. *Gwilt needs to sort his blackout curtains,* Tom thought as they stealthily headed towards the window. The gap was only narrow, and they had to get right up against the window to see through. It was one person at a time. Gwilt and Uncle Fred were sitting on the colonel's huge sofa looking at a sheet of paper. The boys each strained their ears but could make nothing of the conversation.

"Maybe it's a secret map for the next pig rustling?" Tom offered.

"Maybe," John whispered. Philly Brown still had his face to the window, watching what was going on. And nothing much did go on. The two men stayed seated on the sofa, talking about the piece of paper Gwilt held. The boys were getting cold. John was thinking about taking the gang back, and Tom agreed. He didn't think there was much more they would get from that night. They could go back to the house and try to stay awake until they heard Uncle Fred return.

"Wait!" Philly Brown hissed. "Gwilt's got up."

"We're for it if Uncle Fred catches us," Tom said.

"What's he doing?" John said.

"He's gone out of the room. Hang on, he's come back in. He's got that violin with him." The boys were puzzled. Was Colonel Gwilt about to give Uncle Fred a punishment?

Then the sound of soft music. Beautiful, clear music from the violin.

"Is that Gwilt?" John asked.

"Must be," said Philly Brown. "But I can't see him."

"What's Uncle Fred doing?"

"He's just sitting there."

The boys couldn't quite believe what they were hearing. John knew the playing was good, but all three of them wondered how Colonel Gwilt could be so good when he was so awful playing at school.

"Come on," John said. "We'd better get back before Uncle Fred does come out."

Silently the three of them crept away from the window and back on to the driveway. Once they felt they must be out of Fred and Gwilt's hearing range, especially as the music was still playing, they broke into a run down the colonel's drive. But John suddenly stopped, putting his arms out and catching Tom and Philly in their chests.

"Stop. Look over there."

Panting, Tom and Philly Brown looked to the right where John was pointing. They could see a group of people standing in the far corner of the field next to them. It was Colonel Gwilt's field where he kept his pigs. They would all be in their sties sheltering from the cold.

"Who could that be, our Tom?" But Tom couldn't answer his brother's question. It was hard to make out even how many there were.

"Quick, crouch down, military training," John said. "Philly, keep looking back up at the house in case Uncle Fred comes out."

The boys skulked down the driveway, thankful that there was a hedge to hide them. They came to a wooden gate, close to the corner of the driveway and the lane and were just about level with the group, who were on the far side of the field. Philly Brown was looking back up the driveway for any sign of Uncle Fred. John and Tom peered through the gate.

"Recognise anyone, our Tom?"

"No. They're still too far away."

"I reckon we try to get a bit closer. It might be the pig rustling gang," John Boden suggested.

"I don't think we should, our John. Uncle Fred could come out of Gwilt's at any moment. They might just be some gamekeepers, and that would mean they've got guns." John knew his brother was right. He made a snap decision.

"Any sign, Philly Brown?"

"None."

"Right, back to the farmhouse and keep your heads down. This is getting far too serious."

The boys broke into a crouching run to get to the lane as quickly as possible without being seen. At the junction they looked towards the group of people in the field but couldn't see them, so that meant the group couldn't see the boys either. John looked back up at Gwilt's mansion. It was higher up than the lane, so when Uncle Fred did come out, he would probably be able to see them running along the lane in the bright moonlight. There wasn't a moment to lose.

"Fast as you can," John said. "Back to the farmhouse." The three of them sprinted off towards the bend in the lane. "You two keep going, I'll be along in a second," John added as they reached the oak tree.

Tom and Philly Brown did as they were told. Tom because he was terrified, and Philly because he was happy to do as he was told.

John took one last look up the lane but could see nothing. He looked along Gwilt's driveway all the way up to the house but, again, nothing. They were in the clear. He sprinted after the other boys.

They went back into silent mode as they approached the back door of the farmhouse. They couldn't risk waking Molly Bytheway up. Tom went to Ella again to calm the excitable collie down.

"Boots off," John said as they quietly closed the back door behind them. "We can't walk snow and mud through the house. And we'll be quieter in our socks."

The boys crept through the house and up into their bedroom. Their hearts were still racing, and each could hear the blood pumping in their ears. John stopped at the Bytheways' bedroom and put an ear to the door. He heard gentle snoring and breathed a sigh of relief.

When they were back in their own bedroom, he told Tom and Philly Brown to change into their pyjamas while he watched at the window for any sign of Uncle Fred coming back. Tom took over when he was dressed. Then all three of them stood waiting to see whether Fred came back.

They gave up after a while. There was no sign of him.

GWILT'S MANS

THE OAK IN THE BEND OF THE ROAD

John Finds the Pig Rustlers

"What were you lot doing out last night?"

The boys stopped in their tracks, spoons halfway to their open mouths as they sat around the kitchen table eating their breakfast.

"Come on," demanded Fred Bytheway. "I ain't no idiot. Look at your boots."

As one, John, Tom and Philly Brown whipped their heads round and looked at the boots they had left by the back door when they had come in the night before. There was a puddle of muddy water; the melted snow that John told them not to walk through the house.

"Well?" Fred Bytheway looked furious. And as a big man, when he was furious, he was terrifying.

"We wanted to test out my magic torch," Tom said, quickly. It was all he could think of to say.

"Is that right? Well you can give me that magic torch, Tom Boden. You'll not have it again until I think you boys have learned a lesson. Any number of people out at night round these here parts. You could have been shot by a poacher. Or a gamekeeper. Or come across that rustling gang they still ain't caught. You understand?"

Three heads nodded slowly. John and Philly Brown were thinking the same thing; have we got away with it? Uncle Fred didn't seem to know they had been following him. Tom was just thinking about his magic torch. He'd only had it a day and he'd lost it already.

"When you've finished your breakfast, go feed the beasts. Afterwards get in the barn and give it a bloody good clean. After that come and find me and I'll give you summat else to do. Me and our Molly are here to look after you. If you go out at night, we can't. You ain't never going out at night again, you hear?"

The boys ate the rest of their breakfast in silence. They had only ever seen Fred Bytheway this angry once before when he found them playing with a box of matches in the barn. They hadn't thought it was really dangerous and that the hay could catch fire really easily. They had just been playing. They all hated being told off, especially when they weren't being deliberately naughty. Fred had worked them hard that day. He was doing the same now.

Molly Bytheway had her hands in the sink, washing up. She was secretly proud of how her husband dealt with the boys. He would have been a great father. If only she could be a mother.

*

The boys put their boots on and went outside. They didn't dare look at either of the Bytheways in case Uncle Fred got angry again. John went off to sort out the pigs, Philly Brown the sheep. Tom got the bird feed but didn't take much care as they busied around him. His torch was gone. And he loved it so much.

The Bodens never had much. They were a poor family and there were a lot of them. Mam and Pop would have broken the bank to pay for the presents they had given their children that Christmas. It wasn't fair.

He kept thinking back to the night before. To Fred Bytheway secretly meeting Colonel Gwilt.

What was on that sheet of paper they were looking at so closely? Could it have been a plan to rustle a pig? Or maybe something worse. Maybe the rustlers had got bored with just pigs. Maybe they were looking at bigger crimes that needed more planning?

But why the music? Why, after plotting like that, would he then listen to a man playing the violin? A man who pretended he couldn't when he was being headmaster of his local school. Philly Brown said he couldn't actually see Gwilt playing; he was hidden by the blackout curtains, but he saw him walk in with the violin. Maybe it was a record that he had put on? Or the wireless? No. Colonel Gwilt could play the violin properly and Fred Bytheway had sat there and listened.

The Bytheways never seemed to have much to do with the colonel. Fred even deliberately poached rabbits off the colonel's land when there was no need to. He went on about the landed gentry having too much of the pie. And yet he was round the colonel's house in the middle of the night, looking at God knows what and listening to the violin. It didn't make sense.

Then there was that group of people at the bottom end of Colonel Gwilt's pig field. The boys couldn't tell how many there were but certainly more than three. Did Gwilt have that many gamekeepers? And would poachers be that obvious? It had been a very clear night and the moon had shone brilliantly. It was almost like daylight once you were outside. And the snow sparkled and reflected so everything was lit up.

It was a miracle they hadn't been seen but so stupid of them to leave their boots like that. They should have dried them off first, but they thought Uncle Fred might return at any minute. They had made mistakes.

If it had been enemy territory they would have been captured. Tom could kick himself he was so annoyed. And then he thought yet again about his torch and could have cried.

Ducks and geese fed, Tom put the feed away and traipsed over to where Philly Brown was surrounded by hungry-looking sheep wrenching hay from his hand. He'd thrown a load on the ground where it settled on the snow, but the sheep were only interested in what he was holding. Tom knew the little cuts would be opening up again as Philly handled the rough hay. Ella was by Tom's side, but the sheep didn't seem to care. It was as if they knew when the sheepdog was on duty. Right now, she wasn't.

John came over from the pig field. He'd become very good at keeping just out of range of the boars, especially the one that attacked him a few months earlier. Looking after farm animals, or husbandry, as Uncle Fred called it, was not that hard, really. There was just so much of it to do all the time. Farming was a hard job, and it didn't matter what the weather, you had to be out in it doing your work. John and Tom looked on as Philly Brown finished.

"Barn!" Fred Bytheway shouted from the back door. They didn't realise he had been watching them. They walked slowly, heads down, each of them lost in his own thoughts about what had gone wrong.

After Christmas Day with their parents, and the excitement of the day and night before, this day was turning into a horrible one. John and Philly Brown raked up the loose straw and Tom put it in a wheelbarrow. It was his turn to have his hands shredded. When the wheelbarrow was full he would take it to the edge of the sheep field and leave it in a pile.

The sheep might nibble at it, but mostly it would rot there. On his second trip, Tom saw Fred Bytheway coming out of the house.

"When that barn's done, I want you to do the other two."

Tom looked at Uncle Fred's other two outbuildings and nodded sadly. Looking satisfied, the farmer walked out of the yard and turned right. He was going up the lane again, the same way he had gone the night before.

*

"He's off again," Tom panted.

"Who?" asked John.

"Uncle Fred. He's off up the lane towards Colonel Gwilt's again. Something is definitely going on."

"Should we follow him again?" Philly Brown asked, but Tom shook his head.

"Philly, go back to your sheep field and pretend to be feeding them," John said. "You should be able to see if he walks up Gwilt's driveway from there. It won't look like we are watching him."

"I don't know, our John," Tom said. "We're in enough trouble already, and he's just said we've got to do the other buildings as well."

John groaned. At this rate it would be dark before they'd finished.

"I've been thinking," John said. "We need to speak to Meg about this. She might be able to help. We've got our evidence. It's weird he went to Gwilt's and then there was that group in the field. I think we need to see what she says." Tom and Philly Brown agreed.

"Then we'd best get a move on if we're going to finish this lot in time." Tom was always the sensible one. They didn't mind hard work, but now they had a reason, they worked much faster. But instead of Philly Brown pretending to feed his sheep they decided Tom would look out for him when he took the next wheelbarrow of waste out. He scanned Colonel Gwilt's driveway but couldn't see him. Did that mean he wasn't visiting the colonel at all? If not him, then who? There was only the Hoggins' farm farther that way, and Uncle Fred didn't seem to have much time for him.

*

The boys cleared the barn and the other outbuildings in double quick time. They were exhausted, but they could find Meg and talk to her.

"Aunt Molly," John said, a little nervously, "can we go and play now? We've done everything Uncle Fred asked of us."

Molly Bytheway looked down at the boy. She was trying hard to look stern, as if she were as angry as her husband that the boys had sneaked out. She nodded without speaking because if she had, she would not have been able to look angry. John beamed. "Thanks!" he said and rushed out, straight into the broad chest of Fred Bytheway.

"Where you off to then?"

John was suddenly very worried. "We've fed all the animals and done all the buildings, just like you said, Uncle Fred. And so I asked Aunt Molly if we could go and play because you weren't here."

"I'm here now," Fred Bytheway said. "I'm gonner check on them buildings before you go anywhere."

But the boys had been clever. They knew if they didn't do a good job, they would be told to do it again. With it getting dark so early, they were up against time if they were to find Meg and tell her all about what had happened. Fred Bytheway looked around, impressed. The barn was as spotless as it ever got and so were the other outbuildings.

"Off you go," he said at last. "But back before dark, you hear me?"

"Thanks, Uncle Fred," the boys said as one and they shot off towards the football field. Except they ran straight past it, even though there was a game on, and carried on to the Bettons' house.

Lily Betton told them Meg, Chrissie and Mary were down in Meg's den, so the boys rushed through the Bettons' back garden and out into the woods. By then, they knew exactly where Meg's den was and found it immediately. Meg was reading a story to Chrissie and Mary, but she stopped as soon as she saw something was up with the boys. John told her what had gone on the night before, with Tom or Philly Brown jumping in if he forgot something. Chrissie and Mary listened quietly. They realised quickly that John thought this was serious, so didn't interrupt.

"You're wrong about Fred," Meg said. "I just know you are. It's strange that he's going out late at night, though."

"But Colonel Gwilt can play the violin really well," Philly Brown added. "What's all that about?"

"Yeah, that's odd as well. I've only ever seen him do the screeching thing," Meg agreed. "But he's a good man is the colonel. My mum says so."

"What about that group in the colonel's field?" Tom asked. Meg thought for a moment. That was oddest of all. "Could it have been gamekeepers?" Tom persisted.

"It could, but he's only got two. You said there were more." The boys nodded. Chrissie listened carefully. She held on to her doll, which she had decided to call Matilda, and stroked its hair. Mary was getting bored.

"Maybe I could climb into Colonel Gwilt's house and find the piece of paper?" Everyone looked at Mary. "What? I've done it before," she added defensively.

"You've been in the colonel's house before?" Meg asked, stunned.

"No!" Mary replied. "But I've climbed through windows before. I'm good at it."

John Boden was thinking. It could be a good idea, but it was dangerous. Meg was shaking her head. Tom was thinking what Meg was clearly thinking. It was too dangerous, and they'd really be for it if they got found out. But John was their leader and it was his decision.

"I could break in," Philly Brown suggested.

"But that's my job, Philly Brown," Mary argued. "And it was my idea."

"We'd have to watch the colonel's house and then sneak in when we knew he was out," John said, thinking aloud.

"It's a bad idea," Meg insisted. Tom agreed but stayed silent. "And how would you know it was the right piece of paper?" Meg added. John nodded. That was a fair point.

"I don't know," he said. "But we've got to do something. There is something not right about all this and, as Uncle Fred said earlier, they still haven't caught that pig rustling gang."

"He's not part of it," Meg said firmly. "I'm telling you."

"You've convinced me," John said, lying. "So what do we do?"

126

Meg said they should do nothing as Uncle Fred and Colonel Gwilt were not criminals. She also said that if they did find the pig rustling gang they would probably get hurt. Or worse. She let that hang in the air for effect. It worked on the Conyers Street Gang. Every one of them realised how dangerous it was to try to tackle criminals. All except John, who decided it was what the government would want them to do. But he kept his thoughts to himself.

"We'll leave it," he said. "There's nothing we can do." It wasn't like John Boden to turn down a challenge. Tom was surprised he said it.

"It's getting dark," he said. "Maybe we should get back. We don't want Uncle Fred to be angry with us again."

*

In fact, it was quite dark when they got back, but not totally, so the boys felt they had done what Uncle Fred had told them. As it was, the farmer wasn't in the house and Aunt Molly was quietly knitting in her chair by the fire.

"I've made sandwiches," she said. "They're on the kitchen table."

The boys thanked her and went back into the kitchen to find the sandwiches lying under a tea towel.

"Leftovers again," Tom complained, quietly. "Who puts carrots in a sandwich?"

"Shut up, our Tom, we've got thinking to do," John Boden said between mouthfuls. He liked his food and didn't mind eating the same dinner every day.

Tom was a fussy eater, though, and picked the carrots out. Philly Brown had them.

After they had finished eating they went up to their bedroom.

"I'm not having it," John said. "Something's all wrong here and I want to know what it is. Uncle Fred might not be a pig rustler, but we don't know. Seems like everyone here has loads of food and they are happy to have it when our mam and pop don't. That's not right." Tom and Philly Brown completely agreed. Meg might have been right about Fred Bytheway, but the situation wasn't right, and the boys knew they had to investigate and do whatever they could to find out exactly what Uncle Fred was up to with the colonel, just in case it was to do with the rustling.

"We're going to act normal tonight," John continued, "then we wait to see if he goes out again. If he does, we follow him again." Each time the boys talked about what was going on, and what they were going to do, it sounded more and more serious. But they all agreed. John was brave. So was Philly Brown, and he would have run through walls if John had said so. Only Tom had real doubts, but he would do as John asked.

If he was being completely honest, Tom was convinced Uncle Fred had nothing to do with the rustling. It made no sense to be plotting with Colonel Gwilt when he didn't seem to like him very much. And going out so late at night to meet him was really strange. Maybe they had just never noticed before? But Tom was sure they would have. The masses of food was the one thing that bothered him. That didn't add up. As Alf Betton had said on Christmas Day, it was there if people wanted it. But it wasn't there in Liverpool and that annoyed him.

Fred Bytheway came back around eight. The boys were in the living room putting the finishing touches to Philly Brown's Meccano set. The wireless had been on all evening as Aunt Molly continued her knitting. John turned it off and played his mouth organ again. It was incredible he had only had it two days, he was so good.

"Torch, Tom," Fred Bytheway said as the boys headed up to bed. Tom's heart sank. He was beginning to think Uncle Fred had forgotten about taking it, but clearly he hadn't. He fetched it down from his bedroom and handed it over.

"You'll get this back when I know you three can behave."

Tom nodded. He was really upset. "Up you go, lad. See you tomorrow."

*

As with the night before, the boys lay silently in bed listening out for the Bytheways coming up the stairs and perhaps Uncle Fred heading back down. They did, and he did. He was going out again. The boys burst into action when they knew he had left the house and tiptoed down the stairs. The back door was locked. It was never locked. They tried the front door but that was locked as well.

"He's definitely up to something," John said. "We'll climb out of a window." The boys crept around downstairs trying every window in the kitchen and the living room. They were all locked or painted shut.

"We can get out through our bedroom window," Tom said.

"Brilliant," John agreed, "and we can jump off the porch."

Tom opened the window quietly opened and John, as leader, went first. He carefully put his feet on the sloping roof of the porch and held on to the window for support. Then he launched himself into the night, landing with a bit of a bump softened by the snow on the ground.

Philly Brown went next and did a little roll when he landed. He was suddenly covered in snow, but he hadn't felt a thing.

Tom went last. He had watched the other two and it seemed they had done it so easily. But he was nervous as he climbed out and found the porch roof really steep and difficult to stand on. He counted, one, two, three, in his head and then launched himself.

Except instead of going up, he went down, crashed onto the roof of the porch, slid down and went over the edge, landing on his side.

John and Philly Brown rushed to him. Ella barked once from her kennel.

"You okay, our Tom?" John said, concern etched on his face.

Tom lay still for a moment, trying to work out where it hurt. It seemed to be all over.

John and Philly Brown looked on as Tom tried to sit up. He could but was struggling to breathe.

"I think I'm winded," he said. "You two go on without me."

John listened. Tom had made a bit of a racket when he fell, and Ella had barked, but John decided it wasn't loud enough to wake Aunt Molly.

"Come on," he said, looking at Philly Brown. "Let's go. Tom, get yourself back in the house. I'll need you fit for tomorrow."

John and Philly Brown were halfway down the lane when Tom remembered the house was locked. He hurt too much to climb back in. What was he going to do?

*

John and Philly Brown sprinted down the lane. They barely stopped at the bend with the oak tree, or at the junction with Colonel Gwilt's driveway. They were certain they knew where Uncle Fred had gone and he had loads of time on them.

They took nothing like the care they had the night before, and they were breathless as they approached the colonel's mansion. The same chink of light came through the window and when they crept up to it, they again saw Fred Bytheway and the colonel seated on the sofa looking over what looked like the same piece of paper.

As John watched, the colonel handed the sheet to Uncle Fred, who put it on the coffee table in front of them and wrote something down. He handed the sheet back to the colonel, who looked at it and nodded. *God! What's on that sheet?* John thought.

This sheet of paper seemed as fascinating to the colonel and Fred Bytheway as it did to John Boden. Philly Brown took a turn looking and he watched as the two men continued pointing and staring at it.

"We should have brought Mary with us," Philly Brown said. "We need to see what's on that sheet."

"It's a plan, I know it is," replied John. "It's a plan to steal a pig from somewhere. We don't need to see it, we just need to tell someone about it."

Philly Brown put his ear to the glass and listened as hard as he could, then cupped his ear to see if that helped. He could hear voices, but he couldn't make out anything of what was said.

And before long the violin came out again. That he could hear, just like he had heard it last night. Sweet music coming from Colonel Gwilt's living room as Fred Bytheway listened on.

"We'd better go," said Philly Brown. "I think Uncle Fred's about to leave."

The boys hurried away and made their way down the colonel's long drive carefully. They were worried the group they had seen before in the colonel's field might be about. It was darker, and there was more wind.

Occasionally the moon would peek out from a passing cloud and light up the snow-laden fields. There was a group! And it was at the bottom of the colonel's driveway. Their escape was cut off.

"Quick," John said, and climbed over the wooden gate into the colonel's field. "Follow me."

Philly Brown did as he was told. He was frightened as they sank to their shins in the fresh snow. John Boden led the way as they got nearer to where the group was standing and talking. They heard their voices and snatched a few words as they got closer. John stopped, pointed and whispered.

"If we stay here, Philly, we might get seen by them or by Uncle Fred. We need to make it to that pigsty and get in it."

Philly Brown nodded. John Boden waited for the clouds to cover the moon again and then sprang into action – he bent low, half walking, half hopping through the snow to the entrance of the pigsty.

I hope it's empty, he thought as they got close. Or that it's got a sow not a boar in it. It was empty, but there was straw in it and they crept inside.

It didn't look as though any of the group had heard or seen them, but John and Philly Brown held their breath as much as they could just in case.

They heard voices in the silent air but could not see anyone from where they were lying. The group was in the lane, and there was a hedge between them and the boys.

"Gettin' a bit serious ennit?" one man in the group said loud enough for the boys to hear.

"Yeah," said another, "but in this weather there ain't gonner be anyone out and about. It's too cold. I reckon it's the perfect time for us to do another one."

"So we do this last one, tomorrow night, and then that's it?" someone else said, younger sounding than the other two. *How many were there?* John thought.

A fourth voice, or was it one of the ones they'd already heard? "Things are getting a bit hot around here. I don't think we should do any more for a while after this. People are getting suspicious."

John gasped. They had found the pig rustling gang!

"I needs this." It was the first man again, although John and Philly Brown found it hard to tell as the local accent made everyone in High Hatton sound much the same. "Things are getting a bit tight, if you know what I mean. If we do this one, then things'll be better for a good while yet. We just need to decide when, and where."

"Like we said, we'll do it tomorrow night. It'll be dead easy." Was it the younger one? John couldn't tell.

"Won't use the van this time, though, we'll use my trailer. Reckon it would be too noisy here." That was definitely the older man.

"We gonner push it all the way back?" Someone whistled. To John it sounded like there were four of them talking now.

"Don't be soft, lad, they don't weighs much when there's all of us pushing."

John was thinking fast. There was to be a pig rustling tomorrow night. Just like all the others that had happened on the Hoggins' farm. What was more, Uncle Fred and the colonel were in the clear. Fred was still up at the mansion. As soon the group left, John was going to head back up there and tell them.

"Someone's coming." John made out the shapes of men as they shuffled off up the lane away from the village.

The moon came out. Was that Yapp? Or Yale? He definitely saw Rickers. Blimey, he had known the pig rustlers all along. Well, some of them at least. He saw three of them rush up the lane, but he was sure there had been a fourth.

"Evenin'," said Uncle Fred.

"What you doing out at this hour, Bytheway?"

"Arr don't be like that, just out for a friendly stroll is all." The two men laughed.

"It's a grand night to be out," Uncle Fred continued. "Best time of the day to go for a walk. Clears the mind it does."

"True enough," said the other. "Been up to old Gwilt's then?"

"Oh no, no. I just likes walking on his land. He's got too much as it is."

"You'd better watch out for his gamekeepers, then. Don't want you getting shot, do we?" The men laughed again. John thought there was something familiar about the other man's voice, but he couldn't place it.

"Well," Uncle Fred said. "Don't wanna be keeping you. No doubt I'll be seeing you same time tomorrow night?"

"I reckons you will," said the other.

John couldn't believe what he had heard. Uncle Fred was in on it after all. And that meant Colonel Gwilt was as well. What was he going to do now?

He still couldn't see anything, but he thought Uncle Fred must have headed back to the farmhouse. The other stayed where he was. John was desperate for him to move so he and Philly Brown could at least get back to their beds.

"Did you hear that?" he whispered. But there was no reply. Philly Brown had fallen asleep.

John was tired as well, but he forced himself to stay awake. They couldn't stay out there all night. He willed the man to move, but he wouldn't. John's eyes started to close.

*

Tom Boden woke with a start. He was freezing. The barn got really hot in the summer, but no amount of straw made him warm that night. He had no idea what time it was, but he had to get up.

Surely Uncle Fred had unlocked the door when he had come back from Colonel Gwilt's the night before. That's if that was where he had gone.

Tom gasped as he tried to get up. He'd hurt his side when he fell from the porch. He was desperate to find out what had happened but was really worried that Uncle Fred knew he had not slept in his bed.

He hoped John and Philly Brown weren't too worried when they had found him missing. It would have been just like John to have gone straight back out again as a search party.

They would have checked Meg's den probably, but surely he would have thought to check the barn as well? It seemed the obvious choice to Tom when he realised he couldn't climb back in the night before.

Maybe he had buried himself too deeply in the straw to be seen.

And Uncle Fred had the torch, so they wouldn't have been able to shine a light. He winced again. Had he broken some ribs?

It would make sense because he knew that hurt. Pop had fallen off a roof once and was in pain for ages. He'd been all strapped up, but the worst part, he said, was when he laughed.

That had been a mistake. Sarah, Winnie and Kitty all started telling jokes and Mam only half told them to stop. They found it very funny, even if Pop didn't.

Tom pushed open the barn door. It was still dark, but then it always seemed to be dark at the moment in Shropshire. He wondered if it was different to Liverpool somehow. There were no lights on in the house that he could see, so he decided it was too early even for the Bytheways. That was his chance.

If Uncle Fred had left the door open he could sneak in. Ella watched from her kennel as Tom tiptoed across the yard towards the back door. He tried the handle.

No! It was still locked! What was he going to do now? There was no way he could climb up onto the porch. Tom stood by the back door. He was devastated. He'd never get his torch back now. He looked about him, thinking hard. But it was no use. He couldn't climb and the doors were locked. Did he bang on the door and wake everybody up? That seemed so much worse. He was in for an almighty telling off and he didn't want it to happen any time soon.

He exhaled, felt his side twinge and wandered over to Ella. She was pleased to see him and loved being stroked by him. Tom stood up and walked back towards the lane. He might as well just walk about to try to get warm, at least until first light when he knew the Bytheways would be up and he would have to take his punishment. He decided to head towards Colonel Gwilt's as he was meant to the night before until he fell and hurt himself.

He had made it to the bend in the road by the oak tree when he suddenly heard voices coming towards him. Tom quickly and silently hid behind the tree.

He'd have a hard time explaining himself if it was gamekeepers. Or worse, PC Purslow. What if it was Colonel Gwilt? Or even Uncle Fred? Tom was terrified. But as the voices neared, he could tell they weren't local. They was Scousers. He stepped out from behind the tree and John and Philly Brown leaped out of their skins. Tom laughed, then stopped as he felt his ribs.

"What the hell are you doing out here, our Tom?" John Boden almost shouted once he had got over the fright of his brother appearing like that. Tears ran down Tom's cheeks. His side hurt so much.

"What's wrong?" Philly Brown said, suddenly concerned for his best mate.

"I think I've done me ribs. Like Pop did that time."

John nodded. He remembered.

"What are you still doing out?" Tom asked.

"Long story," John said. "We'll tell you when we get back in the house."

"The door's still locked and I can't climb with my side like this."

"Philly, you can climb. I'll give you a bunk up, then you can let us in. We need to talk about what's happened. Gang meeting as soon as we can." John Boden shivered. He'd been out all night and was frozen.

The boys headed back to the farmhouse. Tom was suddenly more hopeful that they would get away with it. Philly made easy work of getting back onto the porch and through the window with John lifting him up. John and Tom crept round the side of the house to the back door. They hoped Uncle Fred had left the key in the door and Philly Brown would be able to let them in. They got there just as the door opened. But it wasn't Philly Brown. It was Uncle Fred, shaking with rage.

"Get in here, now!" he shouted.

———

137

Grounded!

John and Tom didn't move, even when Fred Bytheway stood to one side.

"Get in!" he shouted again.

"Come away, Fred, they're freezing cold. Look at 'em." Aunt Molly pushed past her husband and put her arm around Tom, who was nearest. "Get yerself in front of the fire, Tom, before you catch yer death. You as well John, quickly."

The boys eyed the farmer warily as they walked past. They both thought they might get a clip round the ear, or worse. Philly Brown knelt in front of the fire, shivering. Molly Bytheway, still in her dressing gown, fussed around the boys. "Fred, put another log on, quickly. You can shout at them when they are all warm. Not before."

Fred Bytheway did as he was told. He was livid, but his wife was absolutely right. Whatever the boys had got up to, they had to get warmed up first. He got the fire going properly and the boys felt its warmth immediately. They could sense Fred pacing around the room behind them. Aunt Molly came in with some hot milk, which they struggled to drink because they were all still shaking so much. Tom turned around. Uncle Fred had stopped pacing and was now in an armchair staring at the boys.

Whatever happened next, it was going to hurt. The cold in their bones eased and the boys began to feel better. They stopped shaking and John felt warm enough to stand up.

He was going to say something to Uncle Fred but he didn't know what.

When he opened his mouth, nothing came out. Philly Brown had stood up as well. Tom struggled because of his ribs.

Uncle Fred pointed to the sofa and the boys sat down. It felt so comfortable after the night they had spent, but none of them leaned back. They knew they were in trouble. They sat up straight as if they were about to get told off by a teacher.

Fred Bytheway stood up. His face was red and Tom could see a vein pulsing in his temple. He was as angry as anyone Tom had ever seen. Even Colonel Gwilt. And he looked enormous looming over them. They were all petrified. He raised a finger, pointing it at each one of them in turn.

"We… welcomed… you… into… our… home."

Molly Bytheway stood, fretting, in the kitchen doorway. She had been impressed by her husband yesterday, but this he took very badly. He hadn't noticed the open window when he came back. But he saw it when he went into their room and found the beds empty. He'd forgotten he had locked the kitchen door and had sat in the living room, with nothing but the glow of the fire for light, waiting for them to come back. He was there when Philly Brown crept down. Philly had yelped when Fred appeared at the bottom of the stairs and shoved him roughly onto the sofa. Aunt Molly had come rushing down and immediately fussed around Philly while Fred went to the back door. All night he had worried about them. It was the middle of winter – and a bad one even for Shropshire. He was more worried they had come to harm, rather than the fact that they had disobeyed him. But now they were all here and safe, he could barely control his rage.

"We wanted to sleep in the barn," Tom blurted out. Fred stopped, his finger motionless in the air.

———

"What?"

"We just wanted a little adventure so we all slept in the barn." Tom knew he was chancing his arm. He didn't know where John and Philly Brown had been, and he didn't know if Uncle Fred knew. But he did know he had to try something, anything, if they were to get out of this without too much bother.

"We're really sorry Uncle Fred. We didn't go anywhere, just the barn. We thought it would be fun and we made sure we stayed in the barn because we knew there wouldn't be any gamekeepers in there. Philly wanted to go to Meg's den, but John said no, because we would have been in the woods and the gamekeepers might have shot at us. It was just an adventure, like."

Tom was rambling, making it up on the spot. He hoped he sounded convincing. John stayed straight-faced as he listened to the lies. Just as he always could. Philly Brown was very impressed. They hadn't even had the chance to tell Tom about the pigsty. They would do that later when they were allowed to leave.

"You went and slept in the barn on a night like last night?" The boys nodded. "Of all the stupid things…"

"We buried ourselves in hay. We thought it might keep us warm," Tom added quickly. "It did for a bit, then we all fell asleep. We know you locked the doors to keep us in. We're really, really sorry."

"See Fred," Aunt Molly said. "Just after an adventure they were. There's no harm in that now, is there?"

Fred Bytheway's rage had vanished. He was still angry, but he was calming down by the second. He was no longer pointing; his hand was by his side. He just looked and looked at the boys wondering what to say.

"You're grounded," he said finally. "For a week." And he marched past his wife and out of the room. They heard the kitchen door slam. Tom looked at the clock on the mantelpiece. It was just before seven. It was early for even Uncle Fred to be going out. Molly Bytheway walked towards the boys. It looked like she might have been crying and they felt very guilty about that.

"He's a very good man, is my Fred. Very good. And you've all gone and upset him like that."

"We're sorry, Aunt—" Tom began but stopped when she raised her hand.

"You need to go back to bed, get some sleep, and think about what you are going to do to make it up to 'im."

Tom and Philly Brown stood up, Tom wincing as he did. John stayed seated.

"Aunt Molly," he said. "What's grounded mean?"

"It means you're not allowed out to play."

John thought about this. "But Uncle Fred can't stop us from seeing our sisters. Can he?" Tom and Philly Brown hadn't considered this.

"I'll make sure they hear you're in trouble and that they have to come here. Now get upstairs, get some sleep and decide what you're goin' a do to make it up to my husband."

*

John quickly retold the story of the night before as the three of them changed into their pyjamas. Tom was stunned. Uncle Fred really was in on it? Meg had seemed so sure. And Colonel Gwilt? Tom just couldn't see it, because Gwilt was so rich and seemed to be the most important man in the village. Like a country squire or something.

John and Philly Brown were really concerned about Tom's ribs. He gasped as he lay down on the bed. Philly wanted to get Aunt Molly, but Tom said no. In seconds he was asleep. John and Philly Brown weren't long after him.

They woke with a start when their bedroom burst open and Meg Betton was standing there.

"What's this I hear of you lot spending the night outside?"

John propped himself up onto one arm. It was light outside, but he had no idea how long he had slept. Chrissie and Mary followed Meg into the room.

"Close the door, our Mary," John said and got a filthy look from his sister for his troubles. But she closed it anyway.

John was rubbing his eyes and sat up in bed. Tom struggled to get up at all. Chrissie and Mary sat down on Philly Brown's bed, but Meg stayed standing. "Well?" she said.

"You're not going to believe me," John said, quietly.

"Try me." Meg Betton was not taking no for an answer. John wondered about telling her everything or keeping the bit about Uncle Fred and Colonel Gwilt out of it.

He decided to tell her the whole story. She didn't move for a long while afterwards.

"The thing is, Meg, what are we going to do about it? You can't tell your dad, because he's best mates with Uncle Fred, and we can't tell Gwilt, because he's in on it as well.

"But if we don't say anything, a pig gets stolen and they get away with it."

Meg sat on the edge of the double bed, squashing Tom's foot under the blanket.

"You are absolutely sure Fred Bytheway told this mystery person that he'd see him tonight and he said this right after those other three walked off?"

"I'm sure, Meg, exact words. 'See you tonight'."

"This doesn't make sense," Meg said. "I really can't believe it."

"Shhh," John said. He could hear Aunt Molly coming up the stairs.

"Knock, knock," she said, without actually knocking. Mary opened the door for her and the woman bustled in holding a tray laden with glasses of milk and biscuits. "Time you boys were up. Get that goodness inside you and decide what you're going to do for my Fred."

Aunt Molly seemed remarkably happy considering. Maybe she just wasn't as bothered as Uncle Fred, or she was relieved that it was nothing more serious than they had tried sleeping in the barn and that wasn't the worst crime she'd ever heard.

"Molly," Meg began, but John shot her a look that definitely said, "No!" "Thanks for the milk," she said, not saying what she had wanted to say.

"Oh, that's no trouble," Molly Bytheway said. "Plenty more where that came from." She bustled back out of the room and hummed as she made her way downstairs.

"You heard that?" John said.

"Heard what?" said Meg.

"Plenty more where that came from. See, there's so much food and stuff round here, everyone must be in on it."

"You better not be suggesting my mum and dad…" Meg threatened.

John threw himself back down onto the bed. It was getting ridiculous. He was accusing virtually everyone in High Hatton.

"I just don't know what to think. You know everyone better than me, Meg, but I heard Uncle Fred say those words.

"We don't have anything like this amount of food back in Liverpool. Mam and Pop can't afford it, or it's too rationed. The war doesn't seem to be happening here. Something just isn't right."

"Do you believe him, Meg?" Tom asked.

"How can I?" She looked up. "Philly Brown, did you hear Fred say that?"

Philly looked a little sheepish. "I heard the group talking, but I fell asleep before they moved off and John heard Uncle Fred talking to the other man. Sorry."

"So we only have your word for it, John," Meg said. John Boden threw his hands up.

"I'm telling you the truth. I don't want it to be like this, but that's exactly what he said. What do you think he could have meant otherwise?"

The Conyers Street Gang and Meg Betton remained silent. Mary was, as usual, getting a bit bored, even though it all sounded serious. She was still annoyed that John wouldn't let her break into Colonel Gwilt's house.

Chrissie stroked Matilda's hair, waiting for someone to say something.

Meg stood up and Tom could move his foot again. "I'm going to see if Ted's playing football," she announced. "You need to do what Molly Bytheway said."

Chrissie and Mary looked at each other. The boys were in trouble and they didn't want to be in trouble as well. "We're going back to our house," Chrissie said as they followed Meg out of the room.

"Brilliant," said John.

*

Dressed, the boys went outside. They heard the sounds of football from the nearby field, but none of them were really in the mood. In fact, Tom almost certainly couldn't play. There was lots of stuff in the yard: the tractor, a couple of trailers. Rakes, shovels, axes. Buckets and rusty old bits of machinery that none of the boys knew the names of or what they did. Any and all could have done with a clean or a tidy away.

"What about that?" Tom pointed to a large iron pot they called the 'sheep cauldron'. "I bet that could do with a clean." One of the worst smells any of the boys could ever remember happened when a sheep died and Uncle Fred would boil its body in the cauldron, which looked just like those ones in comics with cannibals cooking people in them.

"Yeah, that would do it," Philly Brown said. "He knows how much we hated helping with that, it stinks."

The boys got to work. John got in first and used the head of a broken outdoor broom to brush away at the dirt inside. As soon as he got anywhere the smell would waft up and turn him nearly sick. He needed water to do it properly, so the boys decided the best thing was to roll the cauldron on its side and, with just a little water in the bulge, they would take turns to scrub.

When part of it was clean enough, they'd pour the dirty water out, put some fresh water in and then roll the cauldron a short way to start scrubbing the next bit of its insides. None of them were actually sick, even though it was horrendous. *I must be getting used to the countryside,* Tom thought.

Fred Bytheway appeared. Philly Brown didn't see him because he was scrubbing in the cauldron.

"What you doing, lads?"

"We're cleaning this cauldron out," John said. "Aunt Molly said we had to do something to make you see how sorry we are." John kicked at the ground. "We couldn't think of anything worse." Uncle Fred burst out laughing. He'd been furious with the boys all day, but the sight of Philly Brown's bum sticking out of the cauldron changed all that.

"Oh, lads," he said. "You really are good, ain't yer? Come on Philly Brown, get yer head out of that. Yer all forgiven." It had been a great idea of Tom's and it had done the trick. They were so relieved Uncle Fred wasn't angry with them anymore.

"Are we still grounded, Uncle Fred?" John asked.

"No, lad, yer not."

Just then Meg Betton came running into the yard screaming. Ted Edwards was with her. Fred ran over to her. She was almost hysterical. The boys looked at Meg and exchanged worried glances. They'd never seen her like this before. They quickly filed into the house where Aunt Molly started fussing over Meg.

"Wha's happened here?" Uncle Fred asked.

"It's that policeman, Purslow," Ted Edwards said in his drawling Brummie accent. "Meg went over to him, the next thing he cracks her one round the head." They all looked at Meg, who was slowly calming down.

"I told him about the pig theft," Meg said between sobs. John shook his head. He had no idea what was going to happen next.

"When?" Uncle Fred asked.

"Tonight," Meg sobbed. Uncle Fred looked around him. He could see John was really worried.

"Right, wha's goin' on? John?" But John didn't know what to say. He knew Uncle Fred was in on it and now they were about to tell him that they knew. He thought it best just to blurt it all out and hope he didn't get hit for doing so.

"We know about the plan tonight. And we know you're in on it," John said, bravely. Uncle Fred stared back.

"Go on."

"I heard you talking to that man last night. You said you'd see him tonight." Something dawned on John. "Oh my God! You were talking to PC Purslow! I knew I recognised his voice. He's in on it too!"

"John, calm down. From the beginning." It was getting worse. Not only had they lied to Uncle Fred that they had just slept in the barn, but now he was accusing him of pig rustling in front of everybody, including his own wife.

Aunt Molly was looking at her husband. Meg had stopped sobbing but kept rubbing her head where PC Purslow had hit her.

"I was talking to him last night, arr, but not about what you think, John Boden."

"But you said you'd see him again tonight. We know you've been going to see Colonel Gwilt, so we know he's in on it too."

"You need to stop now, John," Fred Bytheway said firmly.

"Yes, I saw Purslow last night. I often do when I am out. And yes, I've been to see Colonel Gwilt a few times lately. But you are completely wrong. I am not involved in no pig rustling."

"But," John said.

"Told you," said Meg.

Fred Bytheway turned to his wife. "This is serious Moll. I'm goin' to take these boys up to see old Gwilt. He'll know what to do. Meg, stay here." He turned to Ted Edwards. "Thanks, lad. We'll take care of her from 'ere."

*

The boys couldn't keep up with Fred Bytheway as he marched up the lane to Colonel Gwilt's mansion. Tom in particular couldn't with his ribs hurting so much. The colonel looked shocked when he answered his door but let Fred and the boys in and led them to the beautiful and huge living room that the boys had seen him and Fred talking in.

"What's that smell?" he said. The sheep cauldron had obviously made John, Tom and Philly Brown stink.

"No time for that, Colonel, got something serious goin' on." The boys decided it was best not to sit on the colonel's furniture. It looked expensive.

Even Colonel Gwilt was shocked as he listened to John retell the story for about the fourth time.

"Rickers? And Yapp?" John nodded. "Or the other one," he said in answer to the colonel's question. "I'm not sure which."

"And you don't know who the older one is," Gwilt persisted. John shook his head.

"Bet you it's Hoggins himself," Fred Bytheway offered. "Too much bad luck for one farmer, I reckons."

149

Colonel Gwilt sat down nodding. He had thought much the same thing over the weeks. Uncle Fred checked himself quickly and decided to stay standing. "Well, I'll be…" the colonel said. "And it's going on tonight?"

John nodded. It was what he had heard. "One last one in the middle of winter when no one was about."

"What you goin' a do, Colonel?" Fred asked.

"I'm getting onto division, that's what. We've a golden opportunity to catch these blaggards red-handed." Colonel Gwilt suddenly sprang into action and left the room. The boys heard him dialling on a phone and speak to whoever was on the other end. They didn't have telephones in Conyers Street, and Tom realised the Bytheways didn't have one either. Gwilt must be the only one in the village. He really was posh. The colonel came back in and stood in front of John.

"So you're the only one who heard all this?" the colonel asked John.

"Yeah. Philly fell asleep and Tom was in Uncle Fred's barn."

"His barn? What was he doing in there?" The colonel shook his head. "That's not important, Wilbur, keep your eye on the ball."

John wondered who Wilbur was until he realised it must be the colonel's first name. The colonel then made him repeat everything he had heard the night before, but John was getting confused. He just knew the group had been talking about doing one last raid because things were starting to look a bit suspicious. Tonight was meant to be that night. When John had finished Colonel Gwilt turned to Uncle Fred.

"And this girl, Meg Betton, she's told Purslow about the raid and that you're in on it?"

"Seems so," said Uncle Fred.

"Then do you think they'll go through with it? Do you think he's that stupid?"

"I think Purslow's very stupid, and very greedy," Fred Bytheway replied.

"Well," continued the colonel. "If he *is* that stupid and greedy, then he will get everything he deserves. A serving policeman committing crimes? Doesn't bear thinking about."

*

Fred led the boys back to the farmhouse. There wasn't much talking going on. Aunt Molly fussed as usual, wanting to know what was happening, so Fred told her.

John offered to walk Meg home, and Fred agreed, warning him to say nothing if he saw any of PC Purslow, Rickers or Yapp or Yale. John promised he wouldn't.

Tom and Philly Brown went as well. Safety in numbers.

"So there's going to be an ambush?" Meg said as they headed out towards the lane. She was much calmer now. She didn't look upset, she looked angry.

"Seems so," John said. "It sounded like same time, same place from what I could hear, so there's a load of police coming from somewhere to hide in the bushes and arrest them all. That's if they are stupid enough to do it."

"Well," said Meg, "he is stupid enough. And now we know he likes to hit girls. I'm going to get him for that."

"You can't come," Tom said.

"Well you are, aren't you?" The truth was the boys hadn't thought about it. John always got stuck in in fights and Philly Brown didn't seem to care for his own safety whenever he rushed in.

Tom usually held back a little but would do his bit. But this was against grown men, or a much larger boy in the case of Yapp or Yale. It would be really dangerous.

"I'm not missing out," said Philly Brown, talking for the first time in ages. "We figured this out, we should be there to see how it all ends. That's right, isn't it John?"

John Boden was put on the spot. It really did sound dangerous, but now Meg and Philly Brown had both said they wanted to see what happened. He felt he had no choice. Tom was instantly worried. They'd already been in so much trouble; there was no way Uncle Fred would let them out tonight.

They arrived at Meg's house to see Lily Betton skipping in the garden with Chrissie and Mary, even though it was quite dark now. She had no idea that Purslow had hit her daughter, because Ted Edwards had forgot to tell her as he was supposed to do. They all went inside, and Meg and John retold their stories. Lily Betton was shocked. She'd be telling Alf Betton the minute he got home from working on the railway. The boys left, but not before Meg had given John a sly wink. He knew she would be out that night to see the ambush. If there was one.

Around the dinner table Uncle Fred was looking very serious. John felt he had to say something to him. He felt uncomfortable that he had accused him of stealing pigs when he now obviously wouldn't and hadn't.

"I'm sorry, Uncle Fred," he offered. "I really didn't want to believe you could do something like that, but you kept going to Colonel Gwilt's and then I heard what you said last night. Meg told me there was no way you'd do something like that but, well, it just sounded like you were in on it." The boys looked expectantly at Fred Bytheway.

"Can't says as I'm too happy, John, but at least you've been man enough to try to explain. Mind you, I think I'd accuse myself if I'd heard what you heard." He put down his fork. He didn't seem to use a knife when eating.

"Right. I ain't gonner say this again, but you lot ain't comin' out tonight, do you hear? If anything does happen it will be really serious and it ain't no place for young lads. If they gets caught, they'll fight bloody hard to escape. I don't want you anywhere near that. I promised your mam and pop I'd look after you. I promised your ma as well, Philly Brown. Me and Molly both did. So that's what I'm gonner do tonight." Fred Bytheway clasped his hands together, forming an upside down 'V' above his plate, and looked at the boys intently.

"You will not go out tonight, cos if you do, and I find out, you ain't gonner know what hits yer. Does I make myself clear?" The boys nodded silently. Uncle Fred could not have been any clearer. Aunt Molly looked disapprovingly on at the boys, as if she knew they would try anyway.

She wasn't as trusting as her husband.

HOGGINS' FARM

The Battle of the Pig Field

Before he went off to see Colonel Gwilt, Fred Bytheway handed Tom his magic torch back. There had been so many misunderstandings and the boys had been naughty, but now the ambush was being set and the boys had tried to apologise, the farmer felt there was no need to punish Tom any further. Tom couldn't contain his excitement. The loss of his torch, even for just a day, had really hurt him. He felt it unfair that he had his Christmas present taken away, but John and Philly Brown had kept theirs.

Uncle Fred had left the farmhouse at eight o'clock. He had given them a final lecture about not coming out or else. By nine o'clock the boys were getting twitchy. They knew Meg would appear outside in the lane at some point and that was the signal for them to get out of the house.

But they had Aunt Molly to contend with. She knew they would try to escape and she also knew there was nothing she could really do to stop them. If they all ran out claiming to need the privy and then disappeared up the lane as she thought they might, the last thing she would do was chase after them making a racket.

If there was an ambush, she couldn't go wading in scaring off Purslow and his gang of thieves. She had also listened to the boys' stories, of sneaking up to Colonel Gwilt's mansion to see Fred through the window, to spending the night in the pigsty with her Fred talking to Purslow just yards away.

Neither had any idea they were being overheard. The boys were obviously good at staying hidden.

A plan had been hatched. Tom stayed in the bedroom, waiting for Meg to appear. When she did, he would go downstairs and go to the outside toilet. That would be the signal for John to come with him and for Philly Brown to go upstairs and climb out the window. It would be too obvious if they all needed the toilet at the same time. Aunt Molly would be suspicious.

This way they had the time it took to go to the toilet and come back again – a few minutes – before Aunt Molly would realise. They would be in their hiding place by then.

Meg appeared in the lane. Tom walked nonchalantly downstairs and announced he was off to the toilet.

"I need to go, too," said John. "Is that all right, Aunt Molly?"

"Course it is, lad. Don't be going off, though."

"We won't," John and Tom chorused. Philly Brown went upstairs without a word. He was out the widow, on the porch roof and in the garden in seconds. Aunt Molly knew it was the great escape and continued knitting. She smiled to herself when she realised they really were using the outside privy as an excuse, just as she had imagined. They were clever lads, but predictable all the same.

But then she thought about the risks. She tried not to worry, and she admired the boys for their determination, but she felt uneasy. She put her knitting down on the arm of her chair and looked into the fire.

"She didn't suspect a thing," Philly Brown whispered as the four of them made their way down the snow-white lane.

They got to the bend by the oak tree and peered around. Nothing and no one was in sight. Tom had said he felt the best place to hide was by a gate just short of where the lane met Colonel Gwilt's driveway. That way, he argued, they would be able to see anything happening at the colonel's house and they could also look further down the lane towards the Hoggins' farm. If anything happened up there they would hear it and maybe see some of it.

The gang crept along the lane and reached the gate. John decided they needed to crouch down in the ditch rather than right next to the gate as that would make them harder to spot.

It made sense. Meg had even brought a couple of blankets; one to place on the ground so they wouldn't be sitting, or kneeling, directly on the snow, and one to cover them up.

"Good thinking," John said.

The problem was, the second blanket was only big enough for two of them at once, so they paired off and took turns.

*

Nothing happened. Not for a long time. The boys kept talking, but Meg would shush them. She was right, of course; they really couldn't jeopardise the ambush.

"Quiet," John said, some time later. "Listen." The four listened hard. Three of them couldn't hear anything. But Meg did.

"It's a van," she whispered.

It sounded as though it was coming from the other side of the ridge along which the driveway to the Hoggins' farm ran across from the lane.

It was because of this ridge that the gang felt they might able to see something happening, because Hoggins' farm was raised up a little, just like Colonel Gwilt's mansion, but the lane dipped down in front of them before rising again, so they had a perfect vantage point. In the moonlight, and against the bright white landscape, the van appeared and turned into the Hoggins' farm driveway.

"I think it's the same one I saw that night I spent in your den, Meg," Philly Brown said.

The van didn't have its lights on, but that was the blackout. No one was allowed headlights on when they were driving in darkness. It caused a lot of accidents, and lots of people were hurt, or even killed, but it meant the German bombers could see nothing when they flew overhead. It saved lives that way.

"It's happening," Tom whispered. "I wonder where all the policemen are?"

"In the hedges around Hoggins' farm, I'll bet," Meg replied. "All the pigs have been rustled from his farm. They obviously think they can do it easily. I think they've got lazy. I'm so glad they're gonner get caught."

The boys agreed. PC Purslow had been absolutely horrible to all of them at one time or another, but he had gone too far when he hit Meg. The boys felt very protective of her, it wasn't good to hit girls. Neither Tom nor Philly Brown ever considered it, but the truth was Meg could probably beat both of them in a fight. It was only John who was stronger.

The rear lights of the van glowed briefly as the driver stopped at the farm. He was too far away to be seen, but it meant the pig theft was on and the ambush would get the thieves. The boys and Meg could hardly breathe.

The excitement didn't last all that long, though; nothing more happened. Not a sound other than owls hooting. "That's a tawny owl," Meg said. "And that's its mate," she added quietly as another hooted back. There was no obvious movement at the Hoggins' farm and, because they could hear nothing from the farm itself, it meant nothing was happening the other side of the farm either, which they couldn't see. The gang grew cold and started to shiver. The time between swapping the blanket between pairs got shorter and shorter. It wasn't much fun anymore.

"Look!" said Meg. She had seen them first. Four black silhouettes slowly making their way across a snowy field. The boys saw them too and knew who they were now: PC Purslow, Rickers, Yapp or Yale and the farmer himself, Hoggins. They all tensed up. It wasn't meant to be like this. The four men were in the wrong field. They were two fields nearer to the village and they were walking straight towards where Meg and the boys were hiding.

"Quick, lie down," ordered John. "Everyone under the blanket. Cover your faces."

It was difficult in the ditch. It was narrow and the four of them could not lie flat next to each other. Tom was at the back and curled up into a ball, feeling his ribs protest. He pulled on the blanket, and felt a kick from John, who was lying in front of him. As the blanket was pulled back. Tom was only halfway in. Philly Brown was next to him and also stuck out the bottom, with Meg's feet in front of his face. John and Meg were lying flat, both of them peeking out from under the blanket as the men came nearer.

They had reached the bottom of the field. There was just a hedge and the lane between them and the four children crouching in the ditch.

Even though his head was buried under the blanket, Tom could hear the crunching of snow under the men's boots. He was terrified. The men stopped and spoke in hushed tones. Tom thought he heard someone strike a match.

"Yer not bloody smoking now, Hoggins, people will see yer fag for miles," Hoggins grumbled. He didn't like being told by Purslow. It had happened a few times, now. The policeman was beginning to annoy him. He was glad it was going to be the last rustling for a while.

"So we all know what to do. Different this one. Gotter be more careful." The sound of Purslow taking charge of the situation grated on Meg. She wanted to get up there and then and attack him for hitting her earlier. She knew she had the element of surprise, but it was true, even with John, Tom and Philly Brown, there was no way she could overcome the four men. She gritted her teeth hard. John could sense she was getting angry. Then more crunching of snow underfoot. The men were on the move. John lifted the blanket and could make out the men were still in the field but walking away from where he was lying down. He lifted the blanket some more. Tom perched up to get a look as well.

"What are they up to?" he said, almost to himself.

"Of course!" John replied. "They mentioned using a trailer for this one. Something about the van being too noisy. How could I forget that?"

Meg and John remained lying down on their fronts, perched on their elbows. Behind them, Tom and Philly Brown had both got into kneeling positions. All of them watched as the shadowy figures disappeared and reappeared through gaps in the hedge. Then they stopped again. The gang heard a gate opening and the men starting to heave and breathe more heavily.

"That's the trailer," John hissed. "They must have left it there as part of their plan."

Horrified, Tom suddenly realised the dangerous situation they really were in. They were perhaps thirty yards from the men, no distance at all, and all the policemen and people like Uncle Fred were the other side of them, staking out Hoggins' farm. The pig rustlers were in the wrong place, which meant the ambush was in the wrong place and, where they were hiding, the boys and Meg were in very much the wrong place.

"We have to stay absolutely still," Tom said as quietly as he could. "If they see us, we'll be for it, and the police won't be able to help us."

The children stayed stock still and watched as Hoggins held up the front end of the trailer and steered it into the lane. Soon the other three appeared pushing the trailer from behind. Hoggins turned the trailer and the four men started to push it down the dip in the lane away from the children. But they were still so close none of them dared breathe. They could still hear the grunts from Rickers, Purslow and Yapp or Yale.

"Where are they going now?" Meg wondered aloud.

"Straight for the ambush!" John said, suddenly relieved. He was sure, had Hoggins turned the trailer the other way, there would be no way his gang would have stayed hidden and not have been seen.

The men seemed to struggle as they pushed the trailer down the dip then up the other side. Then something very strange happened. The turned right into Colonel Gwilt's driveway.

Meg stood up. They couldn't see them anymore from behind the hedge, so she and the boys could not be seen by Purslow and his cronies either.

Cautiously, John, Tom and Philly Brown also stood up, making sure their heads weren't visible above the hedge. There was no chance of that as the hedge was much too high.

Meg took a few steps back and crouched down behind the gate, the boys doing the same. They watched through the bars as the trailer came into view again and the pig rustlers made their way up Colonel Gwilt's driveway.

"They must be after one of Gwilt's pigs this time," Meg said.

"Can they do that? How easy is it to get a pig into a trailer like that?" Tom asked. "Won't it make a lot of noise?"

"Not really. Hoggins has farmed pigs all his life. He knows how to lead them."

"Like a dog?" said John, a bit confused.

"Kind of," Meg replied.

The men were heading for a gate into Gwilt's field – very close to where John and Philly Brown had spent the night in the pigsty. John smiled to himself. There were no pigs in the sty he had slept in. They would have to go to a different one further away if they were to manage to rustle any. But they passed that gate and continued up the drive. A few yards later, the trailer stopped and Hoggins turned it so that it straddled the driveway. The men were next to another gate, one that opened into Fred Bytheway's pig field.

"They're after one of Uncle Fred's pigs," Tom gasped. The gate had been opened and Purslow's lot steered the trailer in backwards. Meg and the boys watched on as they struggled to push against the snow that was deeper there, but they were heading straight for the nearest pigsty.

"Our John," Tom said. "The ambush is in the wrong place. They might not see them."

"You'd think somebody would," Meg replied. "The moon's out." It was true. From where they were, Meg and the boys could see the gang easily against the snow. They were black shadows silhouetted in the eerie white light. The trailer was getting close to one of the sties and, because he fed Uncle Fred's pigs, John knew there was a sow in there.

"What do we do?" Tom asked, getting panicked.

"I ain't having them nick one of Uncle Fred's pigs," said Philly Brown suddenly and he leaped up and over the gate.

"Philly, no!" John shouted, but Philly Brown was running straight for the pig rustling gang.

"Christ," John said to himself and leaped over the gate as well.

"I'm coming too," Meg said, and she was also in the pig field in a flash. Tom stayed where he was. He wasn't sure he could even climb over the gate with his ribs. Philly Brown was shouting at the top of his voice and sprinting towards the now surprised pig rustling gang. John was a few yards behind and Meg a few further back still. Tom was terrified and almost couldn't move. The ambush was nowhere to be seen and his brother and friends were about to fight with four grown men.

Something glinted in the snow the other side of the gate. It was John's mouth organ. It must have fallen out of John's pocket when he leaped over. Tom climbed the gate with difficulty, slipped and landed with a thud, wincing from the pain.

Philly Brown charged straight for the pig rustling gang. He was shouting and screaming as loudly as he could. He sounded like Tarzan. Purslow recovered his wits before any of the other rustlers.

"Rickers, shut that bloody boy up!" he ordered.
Rickers smiled. He recognised Philly Brown as one of the
Scousers always playing football. He liked fighting them.

"Yapp, the other one," Purslow barked. "I've got
the girl," he said more to himself, half smiling. "Bloody
Meg Betton."

Rickers ran straight at Philly Brown. He was
much larger than the younger boy, but the younger boy
was angry. As Philly Brown got near, still screaming, he
launched himself at Rickers, who saw him coming. His
fist crashed into Philly Brown's temple with a sickening
thud, knocking him out immediately. He crashed to the
floor lifeless.

Yapp had caught up with Rickers and they moved
towards John, who was rushing up fast. John had seen
what had happened to Philly and didn't dive through the
air but stayed low and smashed into Rickers' body. The
older boy winced and stumbled in the snow, tripping over
Philly Brown's prone body and falling backwards in a
heap.

Yapp came at John and got him in a bear hug. He
was fat and slow but strong, and John had no chance. He
was choking as Yapp's arm tightened around his throat,
then he was thrown to the ground. Pain shot up his arm
and he screamed. He thought it might be broken.

Meg had reached Purslow. She was determined to
get the evil policeman who had hit her so hard earlier.
And she took him by surprise.

Purslow was ready to catch her and restrain her.
He would hit her a couple of times to shut her up, then
he'd make his getaway. But she didn't run into him. At
the last moment she took off and aimed a two-footed
football tackle right at Purslow's knees.

She caught him absolutely bang on, and the policeman crumpled with a yelp, falling on top of Meg. She twisted to get out from underneath him as Purslow held a knee in agony.

Meg got back up and kicked out at the policeman's chest with all her might. She aimed another one, but Purslow saw it coming and caught her foot, dragging Meg down. He hit her twice, hard, in the head, and she went limp.

Tom watched on in horror. Hoggins had run back to Gwilt's driveway, but Purslow, Rickers and Yapp or Yale were making mincemeat of Meg, John and Philly Brown.

He grabbed the mouth organ and blew for all he was worth. His only thought was to make as much noise as possible. He thought it might sound like a police whistle, but nothing came out. He tried again. Still nothing.

Then he remembered he needed to sort of suck and blow at the same time. He cracked it and he sucked and blew for all his worth. It was like a police whistle. And then he felt the torch in his pocket. He took it out and turned it on waving it around and blowing and sucking frantically.

He looked up towards Hoggins' farm. Torches were turning on. And he heard police whistles, but the noise he made had alerted the pig rustlers and Rickers was running down the slope towards him.

Tom ran to his left. He needed to get as close to the ambush policemen as possible. Rickers changed his angle as Tom ran sideways across him. Tom knew he'd catch him soon, so stopped as quickly as he could.

Rickers shot past him, tried to stop, slipped and smashed into the hedge with a groan.

Tom started to run up the field, blowing and sucking on the mouth organ and waving his torch.

He looked over his shoulder towards the onrushing reinforcements. They streamed down the lane towards the junction with Colonel Gwilt's driveway.

Hoggins had changed direction and was now running towards the village. He was easily caught. Tom expected Rickers to catch him up at any moment, but he didn't. Yapp, or Yale, was now running straight at him, and this time he couldn't get out of the way.

The larger boy hit Tom like a freight train, knocking him flat on his back and winding him. The mouth organ and his torch went flying through the air. Tom waited for the punch, but none came.

He looked up to see Yapp or Yale running towards the gate where the boys and Meg had been hiding. Rickers had got there first and leaped over it, but he fell and one of the ambush policeman caught him as he lay on the ground.

Yapp, or Yale, saw this and changed direction again, now running up and across the field towards the Bytheways' farmhouse. Another policeman leaped the gate and was after him. He was much faster than the fat boy and caught him in seconds.

Tom tried to get up but couldn't. His ribs and back hurt too much. He twisted his head and tried to look for John, or Meg or Philly Brown. He couldn't see any of them.

But he could see PC Purslow hobbling away across the field in the same direction as Yapp or Yale had tried to go. After him was Uncle Fred, catching him with every stride.

He must have come from Colonel Gwilt's mansion, Tom thought, or was part of the ambush.

Fred Bytheway bore down on Purslow and smashed into the back of him with a huge rugby tackle. There was a scuffle, then Uncle Fred punched down once and the struggle was over. The ambush had finished and the pig rustlers had been caught.

Tom lay back and closed his eyes, trying to block out the pain.

*

Fred Bytheway burst into Colonel Gwilt's living room and lay the limp body of Philly Brown on the sofa. He was still out cold. The colonel placed a blanket over him and grabbed at Philly Brown's arm.

"There's a pulse, thank God," he said. "We need smelling salts."

"Molly has some at the farm. I'll go and get them," said Fred Bytheway and he rushed back out.

Next, Alf Betton carried his daughter in. She was holding on to her father's neck for all it was worth, sobbing. Alf lay her down gently on another sofa and sat next to her. She leaned into his protective body and he put his arms round her. The sobs wouldn't stop and tears rolled down her face. Purslow had hit her hard and one of her eyes was closing rapidly.

John walked in under his own steam, but he was crying too. His arm was agony and he really did think it was broken. Colonel Gwilt looked around him aghast. Three children in various states of injury, one of them seemingly very serious. He pulled at his moustache, wondering what to do.

One of the policemen had tried to pick Tom up, but it hurt when he carried him. Instead, Tom had made his way up slowly to the mansion.

Outside the front door stood the pig rustling gang, all handcuffed and guarded by two policemen. Rickers and the one Tom now knew was Yapp looked away as he smiled at them, despite his pain.

Purslow, a huge cut bleeding under his left eye, started as if to try to hit Tom, but he was instantly pulled back by one of the policemen. His face was full of hate for the boy who had got him arrested. Farmer Hoggins just looked terrified and kept dabbing at his eyes.

Tom was shown to a chair in Colonel Gwilt's living room. There were a couple of policemen milling around and it was crowded. Philly Brown wasn't moving as he lay full length on a sofa. John was trying not to move. Tom could see he was holding his arm at a funny angle and guessed he'd hurt it really badly.

Tom then looked over at Alf Betton cradling Meg. She was sobbing and her eye looked awful. Tom felt worst about her. She was a girl, but she had also been the bravest of them all. *This room looks like a field hospital,* Tom thought.

"This reminds me of a Great War field hospital," Colonel Gwilt said aloud to no one in particular. Tom managed a smile but winced a little.

Minutes later Fred Bytheway came rushing in holding a small bottle of something which he passed to the colonel. Gwilt knelt next to Philly Brown, took the lid off the phial and held it under Philly's nose. The boy moved a little, then a lot.

Philly's eyes opened, and he tried to sit up, but the colonel held him down gently. Philly Brown looked about him.

"What happened?" he said so quietly Tom could only just hear him.

"You've been in a little bit of bother, young man," Gwilt said, patting Philly Brown's chest. Philly Brown touched his head. "Ow," he said. Tom hadn't noticed before, but there was a huge egg on his friend's temple. It must have hurt.

Meg's sobs slowly eased. She had been really scared by the fight and the pain from Purslow's punches was getting worse, not better.

John stayed still, reliving the events of just a few minutes ago. The colonel and Uncle Fred fussed over Philly Brown, who eventually did manage to sit up. He left mud from his boots all over the colonel's pale yellow sofa and said "sorry" in his very weak voice.

"Don't worry about that," Colonel Gwilt said with a gentle smile.

Philly Brown was ghostly pale, and the grown-ups were worried about him the most. Aunt Molly and Lily Betton came in breathless. The women looked around. Lily Betton was frantic for Meg and hurried to sit next to her daughter when she saw her. Meg let go of her dad and cuddled her mother.

"Oh, Mum," she said and burst into fresh tears. Lily Betton stroked Meg's flame-red hair and soothed her with gentle whispers that everything was all right now.

Aunt Molly looked down at Philly Brown, concern etched all over her face, then hurried over to John when she was sure there was nothing more that could be done for Philly at that moment. John told her he was okay, but that he thought he might have broken his arm.

"Can you move it?" she asked. John shook his head. "Try." And he did. He winced and shook his head again, fresh tears forming.

"Let me have a look at you, young man," said Colonel Gwilt.

John was scared of his headmaster, but the colonel gave his most reassuring smile and started to feel John's arm.

"Where does it hurt?"

"At the top, near my shoulder." The colonel nodded thoughtfully and gently pushed, trying to decide what John had actually done.

"I don't think you've broken it," he said. "I think it's dislocated. We need to put it back in."

John didn't like the sound of that at all. "No, no!" he said as the colonel took hold of the underside of John's elbow with one hand and placed his other hand on the shoulder. John was petrified.

"Did loads of this kind of thing in the Army. You won't feel a thing, I promise." John screamed as the colonel twisted at the elbow and pushed at the shoulder. There was an audible pop as the shoulder went back in. John fainted from the pain.

"Smelling salts here now, please," Colonel Gwilt calmly stated, holding out his hand. Fred Bytheway handed him the small phial. John came to as soon as the bottle was placed under his nose and suddenly looked confused.

Molly Bytheway had sat down on the arm of the chair that John was in. She stroked his head. "See, the colonel was right. Not broken, just dislocated. It'll be fine, now."

John moved his arm slightly. The pain was still there, but nothing like before. Gwilt had been right.

A woman brought in some hot mugs of sweet tea and the children were given one each. Tom thanked the lady, who he thought might be Colonel Gwilt's housekeeper, admired what he guessed must be the finest china and took a sip.

It scolded him but tasted so good and he hadn't realised how cold he had actually been. Colonel Gwilt stood in the centre of the room, surveying the scene and holding a small cup of tea of his own.

"Yes, yes," he said. "Just like an Army field hospital." Tom wondered what else he was thinking.

Fred Bytheway came over to Tom and knelt in front of him.

"I told yer to stay out of trouble," he said, with mock severity.

"I'm sorry," replied Tom, worried.

"It's fine, lad. But I told yer it was dangerous and look at yer all now."

"Quite right, Fred," Colonel Gwilt said. "But by, I've never seen such mettle as these kids have shown. Never gave a moment's thought to their safety and took a beating. Heroes, one and all."

Fred Bytheway agreed. "And if it hadn't been for that mouth organ, none of us would have known what was going on."

"Were you with the police ambush, Uncle Fred?" Tom asked. "Then why didn't you hear Philly Brown screaming?"

"We did. I didn't know what it was. I thought it might have been a fox or something. They do scream, you know?" Fred said. Tom nodded.

"Then the mouth organ. We were all looking the other way, hidden in our spots, like, and I looked across to where the noise was coming from and there's you waving that torch of yers around. Glad I gave it back to yer now!" Tom smiled.

"That's when we could see there was a fight going on. I knew it was you lot. Knew yer couldn't stay out of trouble. I gave Purslow what for when I saw him hit Meg so hard.

"He's an evil…" Tom saw Uncle Fred's fists clench. "Anyway. He's caused me and Moll a lot of trouble lately, accusing me of rustling when it was him all along. I hope he goes down for a long time."

Colonel Gwilt was exaggeratedly nodding. "He will that, Fred. Magistrates don't look too kindly on livestock rustling, but beating a child? That is much, much worse. He's looking at a very long time in gaol and, as a former policeman, he won't spend his time there easily."

"What about the others, Colonel Gwilt?" John asked.

"Rickers and Yapp are minors, so they will be treated differently. They might be a lot bigger than you, John Boden, but they are still considered children in the eyes of the law. It's up to the court of the day to decide, but I expect them to be sent to a borstal."

Tom looked quizzically at Uncle Fred. "It's a type of prison for older children to go to," Fred Bytheway explained. "So they don't go to grown-up prisons and can get an education."

Colonel Gwilt snorted. "A breeding ground for bullies and psychopaths," he said firmly.

"And Hoggins?" John persisted.

"Hoggins will go to prison and lose his farm. The only good thing for him is that he had the good grace – or should I say *cowardice* – to run the other way when you children launched your banshee assault."

"Where's our Chrissie and Mary?" Tom said, suddenly realising his sisters weren't in the room.

"It's okay, Tom," Lily Betton said. "They were fast asleep when Alf came and got me. I'll go back in a bit to check they're okay."

Fred Bytheway stood up and spoke quietly to Colonel Gwilt. They agreed it was much too late to take the children to a hospital, and the colour was returning to Philly Brown. They decided to use the colonel's Rolls-Royce to take them to the local hospital in the morning.

"You've got a Rolls-Royce?" John asked, amazed.

"Certainly have, young man. You can enjoy the luxury one brings tomorrow." John beamed. He couldn't believe it.

The colonel smiled back at him. He actually rather liked these plucky little children from Liverpool.

COLONEL GWILT'S MANSION

Uncle Fred's Secret

Tom opened his eyes and looked up through the gloom at an unfamiliar ceiling. Ornate shapes in the plasterwork and an enormous lampshade hung down. There were paintings on the wall, of fox hunting or grouse shooting and of stern-looking people from earlier times. *Victorian,* Tom thought.

He raised his head carefully and could see an armchair and a writing desk either side of a window, which had the curtains drawn. He lay back down. He was in the most comfortable bed he had ever known, and the duvet was like sleeping in a cloud. His eyes closed again.

Sometime later, Tom didn't know how long, his door opened. The woman who had brought the hot sweet tea through the night before opened the curtains. Tom strained his eyes when he looked up at her.

"How're you doing, love?" she asked quietly, as if talking to a patient. Tom said he was okay. "Well," the woman continued, "it's getting on for ten now and the others are all up. You should come down for your breakfast. Do you need help getting up?"

Tom pulled the duvet off and tried, slowly, to prop himself up on one arm and then sit up completely. It wasn't easy, and he saw the concern all over the woman's face. But he managed with a grimace and the woman came back from the armchair with a fresh set of clothes.

He was in his pyjamas but didn't remember getting in them. Tom was fine getting in his trousers but needed help to get his vest and shirt over his head. The woman was gentle.

His mouth fell open when, led by the lady, he reached the kitchen door. Colonel Gwilt's kitchen seemed bigger than his whole house back in Conyers Street. Tom realised once again why Pop and Uncle Fred were so into this 'class struggle' they kept going on about.

John and Philly Brown were seated at a huge table, as was Meg, who looked terrible. Her right eye had completely closed, and the skin was shades of red, purple and black. In fact, the whole right side of her face was swollen, and she had a split lip.

Not for the first time Tom's fists clenched at the thought of PC Purslow. Lily Betton sat next to her daughter, stroking one of her hands.

"Hey, our Tom, come and get some of this," John said, happily. In fact, he was the only one who seemed happy. "Oh, that," he replied when Tom asked about his arm. "It's almost fine now, Colonel Gwilt must have been completely right about it being dislocated. As long as I don't move it, I barely notice it."

Philly Brown was not in such high spirits. The lump on the top of his head was the size of one of the Christmas oranges Mam and Pop had brought over. And he still looked very pale. He was trying to eat whatever it was that was in front of him, but he didn't seem to be able to take it down very easily.

"You okay, Philly?" Tom asked, really worried for his best mate.

"Yeah, not too bad, thanks." It was typical of Philly Brown. He always got himself hurt, was always the first one in a fight and didn't care what he was up against, just like last night, and when he came off second best, he never complained. Tom placed a hand on Philly Brown's shoulder then perched himself on an empty stool.

Miss Seabury, as she had introduced herself to Tom on the way to the kitchen, placed a bowl of white gloop in front of him. There was something brown and glossy swirled within it.

"Yoghurt and honey, from the colonel's own bees," the housekeeper said with pride. It did not look nice. Tom took a mouthful and was instantly amazed.

The yoghurt seemed to melt and the honey gave the whole thing an amazing sweet taste. He was instantly convinced and bolted down the rest to get a second helping. He didn't realise how hungry he had been.

"Good! We're all here!" Tom turned too quickly and felt his ribs as Colonel Gwilt breezed into the room. It had been his idea and ultimately decision that the injured children should remain in his mansion for the night for risk of moving them anymore.

There was particular concern for Philly Brown, who seemed so ill, and also for Meg as they watched with horror as her injuries seemed to get worse and worse. Lily Betton had stayed over with her daughter, but Alf Betton went back to look after Chrissie and Mary.

Aunt Molly and Uncle Fred had gone back to the farmhouse once they felt sure Tom, John and Philly Brown were all okay. Miss Seabury insisted she would sit with Philly Brown, while the concerns over Tom and John were much less.

"Time for us to have that ride in the Rolls-Royce!" the colonel said, grandly. Tom had forgotten about that. They really were experiencing a completely different world. He quickly finished his second bowl of yoghurt.

Philly Brown had barely touched his and didn't seem to feel any better when he was given the front seat in the car.

Tom was in the middle of the back seat. Meg said nothing, but John could barely contain his excitement.

The nurses and doctors at the hospital were amazing. The nurses insisted on the children being put in wheelchairs, even though John and Tom could have easily walked and they all had torches shone in their eyes and strange things put in their ears.

Tom wondered if it was the same as an army medical. Each of them went for an X-ray or two and then waited for the results in one of the millions of rooms the hospital seemed to have. They also had photographs taken of all of their injuries.

Colonel Gwilt had insisted on this as evidence-gathering for the cases against the pig-rustling gang. Looking at Meg, Purslow was in real trouble.

Colonel Gwilt was amazing. He told stories of his time in the military, of when he was in the Sudan and natives would spin and jump their way towards the British guns, or South Africa and how the Boers were almost impossible to spot because they were really just armed farmers and knew the terrain so well.

Tom knew he was just trying to cheer everyone up as he remembered the colonel's speech on the first day at school, about war being a damned bad business or something, but this time he was talking about his experiences as if they were adventures.

When the doctor came in, Gwilt instantly stopped and waited for the diagnoses.

John was told he had indeed dislocated his shoulder but that there was no break or obvious damage elsewhere, so as long as he kept his arm in a sling, it should heal naturally over time.

Tom was told much the same. His ribs were cracked, not broken, and would take a bit of time to heal naturally.

Philly Brown had what the doctor called a severe concussion. Gwilt was to keep a close eye on him and bring him back should the headaches Philly was having continued. As it was, Philly Brown started feeling better as soon as a nurse had given him some pills. The colonel was given the bottle and told how often to give them to Philly.

Meg was the one real concern, though. She had a fractured eye socket. Purslow had hit her so hard he had actually broken bone. Tom tensed again. He hated Purslow almost as much as Hitler in that moment. The doctor wanted to see Meg again in a couple of days to check on the swelling around her eye, but she too was given tablets for her headache and seemed to perk up a little.

The doctor motioned for the colonel to follow him out into the corridor. The door remained ajar and Tom sneaked up to listen in. His eyes widened when the doctor mentioned Meg might lose the sight in her eye, although the doctor emphasised that was the worst possible conclusion. His opinion was that she would be fine.

Tom jumped on his chair too quickly as Colonel Gwilt came back in the room. His ribs complained again. He had to be more careful.

"Come then, children, back in the Rolls!" Tom could see that behind the colonel's lively manner, he was deeply concerned about Meg. Tom was as well. He couldn't imagine being blind, even if it was just in one eye. He felt very sorry for her and yet, somehow, even more proud of the way she had tackled Purslow.

She was as fearless as Philly Brown, if not more. He could never imagine Chrissie or Mary doing something like that, but then they were younger, so maybe they would get brave as they got older.

179

The colonel put Meg in the front seat this time. She was clearly his greatest concern. As it was, whatever tablets they gave Philly Brown, they were working a treat, and he was happy in the back with John and Tom. His cheeky, happy smile returned on the journey through the woods and fields of Shropshire, and he started chatting like the old Philly Brown.

Tom decided he could never call Shropshire home, not while Mam, Pop and all his brothers and sisters were still back in Liverpool. Even if they did all come to live in the country, how would he get to watch Everton or Liverpool every week? No, he knew why he was here, but he decided he'd go back to Liverpool tomorrow if he could, even if Hitler was dropping the odd bomb.

An image popped into his head: what would everyone in Conyers Street think if he turned up in a Rolls-Royce? Tom smiled and looked out through the front windscreen as the car twisted, dipped and climbed its way back to High Hatton.

*

It was mid-afternoon, and although still early, brooding clouds and the time of the year were coming together. It would be dark soon. Colonel Gwilt helped Meg out of the front seat while the boys struggled out of the back, each being more careful of the injuries they had.

In the front room were Chrissie and Mary, who rushed up to see how their brothers were. The Bettons and the Bytheways were there as well.

The colonel took Alf and Lily Betton to one side after they had fussed over their daughter and Tom could guess what they were being told.

Lily Betton put a handkerchief to her mouth. Alf Betton looked at his daughter, her face so horribly injured, and took a deep breath.

Tom saw this and hoped he didn't blame himself for Meg sneaking out to watch the ambush. He realised again what children put their parents through. Meg had done just what he and John and Philly Brown had done loads of times in the past, only this time she had got badly hurt. They all had.

Not for the first time Tom realised just how stupid as well as brave they had all been the night before. To make them feel better, Tom sensed, they were only ever told how brave they were. That was until a car pulled up outside and Mam stormed in.

"Stupid!" she shouted at Tom and clipped him round the ear.

"Mrs Boden, please!" the colonel said in his deep and serious voice. Mam stopped. "These children have been incredibly brave, and they have done this community a great service. No, it was not a good idea they attacked that gang, but they showed no thought for their own safety. Please, have a cup of tea. Miss Seabury!"

Mam softened. She looked at Tom and ruffled his hair. "Sorry, son. But I do worry." She looked at John and his arm in a sling and went over to him. Philly Brown was grinning. He seemed perfectly fine, but then Mam saw Meg Betton and failed to keep her shock to herself.

"It's okay, Mrs Boden," Meg said, trying to smile. "I know it looks awful. I've looked in the mirror."

Tom had not got over the shock of seeing his mother. He wasn't expecting her. Neither had John. It was Philly Brown's turn to be shocked when his ma walked and went straight up to him.

"I'm fine, Ma," he protested.

Meg was flanked by her concerned parents by the time Miss Seabury brought the tea in and Mam and Philly Brown's ma were given seats. The colonel stood before them and whispered to them out of earshot of the children. Tom guessed he was recounting the extent of their injuries.

"Is Pop coming?" he asked.

"No," said Mam. "He had to work. And I've had to leave the little ones with your sisters. Again." Tom saw the look and decided not to say any more.

"So if not your husband, who brought you here, Mrs Boden?" Colonel Gwilt asked.

"We came by police car, your Lordship. It came this morning."

Gwilt laughed. "Please, it's just 'Colonel'. Not made my way to the House of Lords just yet!" Tom could see Mam was embarrassed. "Miss Seabury, please can you invite the policeman in? I can't bear the thought of him sitting out in the cold."

Tom's eyes widened as PC Murphy was led in. He was huge, and the boys could never quite tell if he was a goodie or a baddie. He had always been friendly to them in Conyers Street, but Tom thought there was an edge to him and he had seen PC Murphy arrest people and take them down to Athol Street police station. He wasn't gentle then.

It was PC Murphy who had been at the forefront of Tom's mind the only time he stole something. Walking past a greengrocers shop, he grabbed an apple and stuffed it in his pocket. *Just like the Artful Dodger,* he had thought, but then he had started to worry. What if he had been seen? What if it was PC Murphy come to arrest him?

He suddenly broke into a run across Scottie Road and up Conyers Street, but he carried on going. He didn't stop until he had reached Goodison Park, Everton's football stadium. There he hid in one of the doorways that led to the turnstiles and took the apple out.

He kept peering out the doorway to see if he had been followed. He didn't seem to have been, but he was so nervous he couldn't actually eat the fruit. He threw it away and never stole anything again. It didn't bear thinking about being arrested by PC Murphy.

As it was, PC Murphy chose to remain standing in the busy living room and the adults chatted away. Miss Seabury brought in seemingly endless cups of tea as more people arrived. A serious-looking older man in police uniform spoke to Colonel Gwilt at length.

Aunt Molly turned up with Uncle Fred. The adults talked about the ambush the night before. Colonel Gwilt questioned the intelligence they had received and therefore why they had put the ambush in the wrong place.

He had to be reminded that it came from a freezing ten-year-old boy eavesdropping from inside a pigsty. "Quite right!" the colonel exclaimed.

The boys and Chrissie and Mary huddled around Meg. She could talk, but she was fairly quiet. Her head still hurt although she insisted not as much as it had done. But her mouth was swollen and sore and it made it hard to talk.

The children listened silently as she explained how she had managed to floor Purslow. John whistled. Sometimes when things got heated on the football field, boys would try a two-footed tackle to try to hurt their opponents.

Tom didn't like doing it, and hated people trying to do it to him, but the trouble was every time he did actually try, John laughed at him. He would miss and John would say it was because he was too slow. That always angered Tom. John told Meg that he had seen what had happened as he lay in agony in the snow. He then told them what Philly Brown had done and they all thought it so brave.

Philly Brown could remember nothing, not even jumping over the fence and screaming as he ran up the hill towards danger. Tom told the story from his angle. He had seen them all get hurt and explained why he didn't rush in as well.

Chrissie put a protective arm around him. He felt embarrassed, but as John said, without his raising the alarm it could have been much, much worse.

*

"Right," said Colonel Gwilt. "I think it time we have the debrief, don't you?" He had moved to the centre of the room and was used to having people listen to him. He motioned to the serious-looking older man he had been talking to.

"This here is Chief Constable Garbett, a personal friend of mine who has come here to tell you of the police perspective of last night's events. It was he that I telephoned when I heard of the planned pig rustling plot and he who put in motion the ambush that ultimately led to the arrest of two men and two youths. Chief Constable."

"Thank you, Colonel." The chief constable stepped forward.

"Bert Hoggins is to be charged with pig rustling, as are Jacob Purslow, Colin Rickers and John Yapp. Purslow is also charged with child battery." Many heads turned to Meg at this comment.

"He will be in prison for a very long time, given the action and indeed the severity of Ms Betton's injuries. He has been a disgrace to his uniform. Rickers and Yapp, as they are under sixteen, will not be charged with the same offence, although their actions in attacking Philly Brown, John Boden and Tom Boden will be taken into consideration.

"Any magistrate or judge who sees the injuries inflicted on these very brave children will have no conclusion to make but that Rickers and Yapp are bullies of the most heinous kind and would doubtless have gone on to be hardened criminals. We can but hope that they learn the error of their ways when they are sent to Borstal."

A number of the adults murmured their approval. The chief constable continued: "The children are to be honoured at a special ceremony to be convened in the next few days. From the stories I have been told, these children, although perhaps rash, are a total credit to both their parents and their guardians here in High Hatton.

"Meg Betton, Philly Brown, John Boden, I have seen bravery and cowardice in many forms. I have seldom seen cowardice the likes of which Purslow, Rickers and Yapp displayed last night. I have also never heard of such selfless actions as you three did last night.

"I sincerely hope you never do such a thing again, however, as you are all examples of just how brutal and evil some men can be."

Tom was disappointed. He really had tried to help, but the chief constable was not including him in on the raid.

"Tom Boden," the chief constable went on, Tom suddenly pricking his ears up. "You showed courage of a different kind. You displayed an intelligence and quick thinking, the likes of which I have also seldom seen, and I, like Colonel Gwilt here, served in the Great War where many such examples of coolness under pressure have been noted and the men who displayed it rewarded.

"You too are an excellent credit to Mr and Mrs Boden and to Fred and Molly Bytheway, who, I have been told, have been selfless in welcoming you into their home at this very difficult time of war."

Aunt Molly blushed. Uncle Fred smiled, just as Mam was smiling. The chief constable walked over to Mam and shook her hand. It was her turn to blush. He then went around all the adults and shook their hands in thanks.

"Don't I get a handshake, sir?" PC Murphy said, and everyone turned to look at him. "Sorry, just my little joke."

"You can have one if you want one, Constable," the chief constable said, walking over to the huge policeman. "I believe it vital that Mrs Boden and Mrs Brown hear what is being said here. I believe you drove expertly on the way down from Liverpool."

The adults laughed. The children mostly smiled, but they didn't get PC Murphy's joke and they didn't know why the adults laughed at the chief constable's reply.

"Miss Seabury," Colonel Gwilt called. "The rewards, please."

Miss Seabury came back into the room carrying a silver tray. There were six paper bags on it and they could all guess immediately what was in them.

Each child in turn took a bag of sweets from the tray and thanked Miss Seabury. They were soon munching on all sorts of lollies and sweets.

"Don't eat them all at once, we shall be dining shortly," the colonel said. "We don't want you ruining your appetites, do we?"

"Colonel Gwilt," Tom ventured. He had a couple of questions he wanted to ask so that he really did know exactly what had happened over the last few days. "Why was Uncle Fred coming to your house really late every night?"

"Oh, we don't need to discuss that here, do we Fred?" the colonel said.

"Don' bother me, Colonel, I ain't got nothing to be ashamed of."

Gwilt nodded. "Fred here has been coming to me for tuition." The children looked on blankly. "He was not a very good pupil in my school and never learned how to read and write. He is now doing both with my assistance. He is correct in that he has nothing to be ashamed of. It takes a different kind of courage to ask the help of others and I can happily say he is coming along tremendously. Soon he will be able to read for himself the excellent report I will be submitting to our local paper, the *Shropshire Post*."

He might not have been ashamed, but he was certainly a little uncomfortable at the colonel's words and looked down at his feet. A murmur rose in the room as people started to chatter again.

"We thought it was a fancy woman," Philly Brown said, and the room went silent. "Only we don't know what one of those is."

The adults in the room were shocked. Philly Brown's ma could have killed her son there and then. Fred Bytheway put his arm around his wife and squeezed.

"I can tell yer, Philly Brown, that this woman 'ere is fancy enough for me." Tom sensed the tension in the room melt away again. He had an idea of what a fancy woman was and could see why Philly Brown was getting daggers for saying it out loud. He decided to change the subject.

"And Colonel Gwilt, how come you can play the violin really well in here, but not at school?" The colonel smiled.

"Because, Tom Boden, when I am here I like to hear beautiful things, but when I am at school, I need to punish children who are naughty. It is not much of a deterrent to play a beautiful tune to a naughty child. And I cannot abide the idea of the cane. Hurting ears therefore seems to be a perfect solution to a recalcitrant child." Colonel Gwilt seemed pleased with himself.

"Can you play for us now?" Tom asked. He didn't realise it, but it was the single kindest thing he could have said to Colonel Gwilt, who stiffened with pride and instantly left the room to return with his violin.

His audience listened on as the magical notes sang in the air. John got his mouth organ out and, although it was more difficult because he could only use one arm, he joined in with the colonel's music. Chrissie took her cue and stood up, humming along.

Everyone applauded when the moment was over. After such an awful night and difficult morning, everyone's spirits were raised.

Miss Seabury stood in the doorway and, once the applause died down, announced that dinner was served.

"It's roast pork," she said.

Historical Note

Planning for the Government Evacuation Scheme, what would later become known as Operation Pied Piper, began as early as 1938.

Once the war was finally declared by Prime Minister Neville Chamberlain at 11:15 on the third of September, 1939, the evacuation plan was implemented immediately. And it was not just children of school age who were evacuated: of the 1.5 million dispersed in the first three days of war, there were over half a million mothers and young children under the age of five, 13,000 pregnant women, 70,000 disabled people and more than 100,000 teachers and others designated as having crucial roles. Just like the Conyers Street Gang, around 827,000 school-age children were taken from their parents and rehoused in areas considered much less likely to suffer from German bombing. A total of 3.75 million people were ultimately dispersed through Operation Pied Piper.

In real life John, Tom, Chrissie and Mary were evacuated to High Hatton in Shropshire and it is fair to say that the tiny hamlet surrounded by rolling farmland could not be more different to Conyers Street in Liverpool. The Scotland Road area of Liverpool, virtually a slum at the time, was crammed with many thousands of very poor, mostly Irish immigrant, families just like the Bodens. Conyers Street alone, a rather short terraced street, had many times the population of High Hatton. But the children went there and many of the side events depicted in this book did happen.

There was an eccentric headmaster and he did play the violin, although Tom's recollection is that he just liked playing it to the children ("It was murder!") rather than doing it as a punishment as Colonel Gwilt does. John and Tom did stay on a farm and did experience many of the little anecdotes in this book. John was savaged by a boar and Tom did fall out of a tree onto a goat.

There were children from Birmingham and there was a boy called Edwards. The 'dead sheep cauldron' was real and the smell horrendous. Tom was taught to kill the Christmas goose. Water on the farm came from an outside water pump and the metal handle would rip skin off when it had frozen in winter. The shredding of hands handling frozen hay is another distinct memory of Tom's.

My personal favourite, however, is the story about Pop cycling to High Hatton. In real life he did do this on a number of occasions. I have nothing but admiration for a man who works a five and a half day week on the docks at Liverpool before getting on a simple push bike at midday on a Saturday and riding to High Hatton. Online mapping has the distance at anywhere between 56 and 72 miles and taking around six hours. In 1939, and with a much more basic road network, it is likely that distance is higher and would have taken longer. Pop undertook this journey on several occasions and, at times, he would have ridden in the dark given the blackout. He would stay overnight and cycle back the very next day in time for work on the Monday. That is akin to a stage of the Tour de France. On a pushbike. In the dark.

The biggest poetic license outwith the main plot are the whereabouts of Chrissie and Philly Brown. As a child the real Chrissie suffered frequently from a bad throat and tonsillitis. Pop would buy bottles of tonic for her to soothe her throat. In High Hatton Chrissie refused to drink, became ill and got herself returned to Conyers Street. I have kept her in Shropshire long after she had actually left. As far as Philly Brown goes, I don't know where he was evacuated to, or even whether he was evacuated at all (although that is highly likely) but I do know he was not in High Hatton.

Outside of these little glimpses into a forgotten world, the story is very much my own. Crime in the UK went up across the board during wartime as much because there were many more things people could be found guilty of such as fiddling ration books, looting bombed out buildings or falsely claiming compensation for having your home blown up (one man claimed he had lost his home 19 times in three months and received the equivalent of £500 compensation each time. He was sentenced to three years' imprisonment when found out).

It is, therefore, a small step to suggest that pig rustling to sell the meat on the black market constitutes a likely rural crime. As this book shows, the vast majority of people were law abiding, but there are always those who seek to take advantage of a difficult situation. For every Hoggins, there were many more Bytheways and Bettons.

And finally, I have chosen to give the local people of Shropshire traditional Salopian names. Being on the Welsh border, many of the names I found from the census of 1881 are indeed Welsh sounding.

Instead, I have trawled through and used those (non-Welsh sounding) names which I think evocative and add a little colour. So there are Gwilts and Rickers, Bytheways and Bettons, Doodys, Yapps and Yales. I have no idea if there were any in High Hatton at the time, however.

Any mistakes historical are my own, but I hope you forgive them and received as much enjoyment reading this book as I had in its creation.

The Conyers Street Gang will return.

Acknowledgments

Writing is a solitary vocation, but it is nothing without the succour and belief of others. This book would never have seen the light of day without the help and assistance I have received from a number of sources.

I would like to thank my excellent publisher, Eloise Attenborough at Book Bubble Press, for her unceasing efforts to get this book out there.

I am also extremely grateful to my brilliant editor, Melissa Carmean who made sense of some of my ramblings, and Kathryn Washburn who made sure I had actually dotted the i's and crossed the t's.

And I owe a huge debt of gratitude to Nicky Dean for her amazing illustrations that bring this story to life.

I would also like to thank my mother and stepfather, Dawn and Brian Hann, as well as Lucy Thame and Jo Price for their constant and continued assistance and support.

And I give thanks all the others who have provided guidance and suggestions throughout the journey I have been on to get to this point – your kind words have been an inspiration to me. You know who you are.

Michael Thame
www.ghostwriterbooks.co.uk

Printed in Great Britain
by Amazon